SFBC 50th
ANNIVERSARY COLLECTION

The
Forever War

Other Books by Joe Haldeman

SFBC 50th
ANNIVERSARY COLLECTION

The
Forever War

Joe Haldeman

SCIENCE
FICTION
19

First SFBC Science Fiction Printing: May 2005.

Published by arrangement with Avon,
a division of HarperCollins Publishers
10 East 53rd Street
New York, NY 10022

Visit The SFBC at http://www.sfbc.com

ISBN 0-7394-5343-2

Printed in the United States of America.

For Ben and, always, for Gay

Private Mandella

"Tonight we're going to show you eight silent ways to kill a man." The guy who said that was a sergeant who didn't look five years older than me. So if he'd ever killed a man in combat, silently or otherwise, he'd done it as an infant.

I already knew eighty ways to kill people, but most of them were pretty noisy. I sat up straight in my chair and assumed a look of polite attention and fell asleep with my eyes open. So did most everybody else. We'd learned that they never scheduled anything important for these after-chop classes.

The projector woke me up and I sat through a short tape showing the "eight silent ways." Some of the actors must have been brainwipes, since they were actually killed.

After the tape a girl in the front row raised her hand. The sergeant nodded at her and she rose to parade rest. Not bad looking, but kind of chunky about the neck and shoulders. Everybody gets that way after carrying a heavy pack around for a couple of months.

"Sir"—we had to call sergeants "sir" until graduation—"most of those methods, really, they looked . . . kind of silly."

"For instance?"

"Like killing a man with a blow to the kidneys, from an entrenching tool. I mean, when would you *actually* have only an entrenching tool, and no gun or knife? And why not just bash him over the head with it?"

"He might have a helmet on," he said reasonably.

"Besides, Taurans probably don't even *have* kidneys!"

He shrugged. "Probably they don't." This was 1997, and no-body had ever seen a Tauran; hadn't even found any pieces of Tau-rans bigger than a scorched chromosome. "But their body chemistry is similar to ours, and we have to assume they're simi-larly complex creatures. They *must* have weaknesses, vulnerable spots. You have to find out where they are.

"That's the important thing." He stabbed a finger at the screen. "Those eight convicts got caulked for your benefit because you've got to find out how to kill Taurans, and be able to do it whether you have a megawatt laser or an emery board."

She sat back down, not looking too convinced.

"Any more questions?" Nobody raised a hand.

"OK. Tench-hut!" We staggered upright and he looked at us expectantly.

"Fuck you, sir," came the familiar tired chorus.

"Louder!"

"FUCK YOU, SIR!" One of the army's less-inspired morale devices.

"That's better. Don't forget, pre-dawn maneuvers tomorrow. Chop at 0330, first formation, 0400. Anybody sacked after 0340 owes one stripe. Dismissed."

I zipped up my coverall and went across the snow to the lounge for a cup of soya and a joint. I'd always been able to get by on five or six hours of sleep, and this was the only time I could be by myself, out of the army for a while. Looked at the newsfax for a few minutes. Another ship got caulked, out by Aldebaran sector. That was four years ago. They were mounting a reprisal fleet, but it'll take four years more for them to get out there. By then, the Taurans would have every portal planet sewed up tight.

Back at the billet, everybody else was sacked and the main lights were out. The whole company'd been dragging ever since we got back from the two-week lunar training. I dumped my clothes in the locker, checked the roster and found out I was in bunk *31*. Goddammit, right under the heater.

I slipped through the curtain as quietly as possible so as not to wake up the person next to me. Couldn't see who it was, but I couldn't have cared less. I slipped under the blanket.

"You're late, Mandella," a voice yawned. It was Rogers.

"Sorry I woke you up," I whispered.

" 'Sallright." She snuggled over and clasped me spoon-fashion. She was warm and reasonably soft.

I patted her hip in what I hoped was a brotherly fashion. "Night, Rogers."

"G'night, Stallion." She returned the gesture more pointedly.

Why do you always get the tired ones when you're ready and the randy ones when you're tired? I bowed to the inevitable.

"Awright, let's get some goddamn *back* inta that! Stringer team! Move it up—move your ass up!"

A warm front had come in about midnight and the snow had turned to sleet. The permaplast stringer weighed five hundred pounds and was a bitch to handle, even when it wasn't covered with ice. There were four of us, two at each end, carrying the plastic girder with frozen fingertips. Rogers was my partner.

"Steel!" the guy behind me yelled, meaning that he was losing his hold. It wasn't steel, but it was heavy enough to break your foot. Everybody let go and hopped away. It splashed slush and mud all over us.

"Goddammit, Petrov," Rogers said, "why didn't you go out for the Red Cross or something? This fucken thing's not that fucken heavy." Most of the girls were a little more circumspect in their speech. Rogers was a little butch.

"Awright, get a fucken *move* on, stringers—epoxy team! Dog'em! Dog'em!"

Our two epoxy people ran up, swinging their buckets. "Let's go, Mandella. I'm freezin' my balls off."

"Me, too," the girl said with more feeling than logic.

"One—two—heave!" We got the thing up again and staggered toward the bridge. It was about three-quarters completed. Looked as if the second platoon was going to beat us. I wouldn't give a damn, but the platoon that got their bridge built first got to fly home. Four miles of muck for the rest of us, and no rest before chop.

We got the stringer in place, dropped it with a clank, and fitted the static clamps that held it to the rise-beams. The female half of the epoxy team started slopping glue on it before we even had it secured. Her partner was waiting for the stringer on the other side. The floor team was waiting at the foot of the bridge, each one holding a piece of the light, stressed permaplast over his head like an umbrella. They were dry and clean. I wondered aloud what they had done to deserve it, and Rogers suggested a couple of colorful, but unlikely, possibilities.

We were going back to stand by the next stringer when the field first (name of Dougelstein, but we called him "Awright") blew a whistle and bellowed, "Awright, soldier boys and girls, ten minutes. Smoke 'em if you got 'em." He reached into his pocket and turned on the control that heated our coveralls.

Rogers and I sat down on our end of the stringer and I took out my weed box. I had lots of joints, but we were ordered not to smoke them until after night-chop. The only tobacco I had was a cigarro butt about three inches long. I lit it on the side of the box; it wasn't too bad after the first couple of puffs. Rogers took a puff, just to be sociable, but made a face and gave it back.

"Were you in school when you got drafted?" she asked.

"Yeah. Just got a degree in physics. Was going after a teacher's certificate."

She nodded soberly. "I was in biology . . ."

"Figures." I ducked a handful of slush. "How far?"

"Six years, bachelor's and technical." She slid her boot along the ground, turning up a ridge of mud and slush the consistency of freezing ice milk. "Why the fuck did this have to happen?"

I shrugged. It didn't call for an answer, least of all the answer that the UNEF kept giving us. Intellectual and physical elite of the planet, going out to guard humanity against the Tauran menace. Soyashit. It was all just a big experiment. See whether we could goad the Taurans into ground action.

Awright blew the whistle two minutes early, as expected, but Rogers and I and the other two stringers got to sit for a minute while the epoxy and floor teams finished covering our stringer. It got cold fast, sitting there with our suits turned off, but we remained inactive on principle.

There really wasn't any sense in having us train in the cold. Typical army half-logic. Sure, it was going to be cold where we were going, but not ice-cold or snow-cold. Almost by definition, a portal planet remained within a degree or two of absolute zero all the time—since collapsars don't shine—and the first chill you felt would mean that you were a dead man.

Twelve years before, when I was ten years old, they had discovered the collapsar jump. Just fling an object at a collapsar with sufficient speed, and out it pops in some other part of the galaxy. It didn't take long to figure out the formula that predicted where it would come out: it travels along the same "line" (actually an Einsteinian geodesic) it would have followed if the collapsar hadn't been in the way—until it reaches another collapsar field, whereupon it reappears, repelled with the same speed at which it approached the original collapsar. Travel time between the two collapsars . . . exactly zero.

It made a lot of work for mathematical physicists, who had to redefine simultaneity, then tear down general relativity and build it back up again. And it made the politicians very happy, because now they could send a shipload of colonists to Fomalhaut for less than it had once cost to put a brace of men on the moon. There were a lot of people the politicians would love to see on Fomalhaut, implementing a glorious adventure rather than stirring up trouble at home.

The ships were always accompanied by an automated probe that followed a couple of million miles behind. We knew about the portal planets, little bits of flotsam that whirled around the collapsars; the purpose of the drone was to come back and tell us in the event that a ship had smacked into a portal planet at .999 of the speed of light.

That particular catastrophe never happened, but one day a drone limped back alone. Its data were analyzed, and it turned out that the colonists' ship had been pursued by another vessel and destroyed. This happened near Aldebaran, in the constellation Taurus, but since "Aldebaranian" is a little hard to handle, they named the enemy "Tauran."

Colonizing vessels thenceforth went out protected by an armed guard. Often the armed guard went out alone, and finally the Colonization Group got shortened to UNEF, United Nations Exploratory Force. Emphasis on the "force."

Then some bright lad in the General Assembly decided that we ought to field an army of footsoldiers to guard the portal planets of the nearer collapsars. This led to the Elite Conscription Act of 1996 and the most elitely conscripted army in the history of warfare.

So here we were, fifty men and fifty women, with IQs over 150 and bodies of unusual health and strength, slogging elitely through the mud and slush of central Missouri, reflecting on the usefulness of our skill in building bridges on worlds where the only fluid is an occasional standing pool of liquid helium.

About a month later, we left for our final training exercise, maneuvers on the planet Charon. Though nearing perihelion, it was still more than twice as far from the sun as Pluto.

The troopship was a converted "cattlewagon" made to carry two hundred colonists and assorted bushes and beasts. Don't think it was roomy, though, just because there were half that many of us. Most of the excess space was taken up with extra reaction mass and ordnance.

The whole trip took three weeks, accelerating at two gees halfway, decelerating the other half. Our top speed, as we roared by the orbit of Pluto, was around one-twentieth of the speed of light—not quite enough for relativity to rear its complicated head.

Three weeks of carrying around twice as much weight as normal . . . it's no picnic. We did some cautious exercises three times a day and remained horizontal as much as possible. Still, we got several broken bones and serious dislocations. The men had to wear special supporters to keep from littering the floor with loose organs. It was almost impossible to sleep; nightmares of choking and being crushed, rolling over periodically to prevent blood pooling and bedsores. One girl got so fatigued that she almost slept through the experience of having a rib push out into the open air.

I'd been in space several times before, so when we finally stopped decelerating and went into free fall, it was nothing but relief. But some people had never been out, except for our training on the moon, and succumbed to the sudden vertigo and disorientation. The rest of us cleaned up after them, floating through the quarters with sponges and inspirators to suck up the globules of partly-digested "Concentrate, High-protein, Low-residue, Beef Flavor (Soya)."

We had a good view of Charon, coming down from orbit. There wasn't much to see, though. It was just a dim, off-white sphere with a few smudges on it. We landed about two hundred meters from the base. A pressurized crawler came out and mated with the ferry, so we didn't have to suit up. We clanked and squeaked up to the main building, a featureless box of grayish plastic.

Inside, the walls were the same drab color. The rest of the company was sitting at desks, chattering away. There was a seat next to Freeland.

"Jeff—feeling better?" He still looked a little pale.

"If the gods had meant for man to survive in free fall, they would have given him a cast iron glottis." He sighed heavily. "A little better. Dying for a smoke."

"Yeah."

"*You* seemed to take it all right. Went up in school, didn't you?"

"Senior thesis in vacuum welding, yeah. Three weeks in Earth orbit." I sat back and reached for my weed box for the thousandth time. It still wasn't there. The Life Support Unit didn't want to handle nicotine and THC.

"Training was bad enough," Jeff groused, "but *this* shit—"

"Tench-hut!" We stood up in a raggedy-ass fashion, by twos and threes. The door opened and a full major came in. I stiffened a little. He was the highest-ranking officer I'd ever seen. He had a row of ribbons stitched into his coveralls, including a purple strip meaning he'd been wounded in combat, fighting in the old American army. Must have been that Indochina thing, but it had fizzled out before I was born. He didn't look that old.

"Sit, sit." He made a patting motion with his hand. Then he put his hands on his hips and scanned the company, a small smile on his face. "Welcome to Charon. You picked a lovely day to land, the temperature outside is a summery eight point one five degrees Absolute. We expect little change for the next two centuries or so." Some of them laughed halfheartedly.

"Best you enjoy the tropical climate here at Miami Base; enjoy it while you can. We're on the center of sunside here, and most of your training will be on darkside. Over there, the temperature stays a chilly two point zero eight.

"You might as well regard all the training you got on Earth and the moon as just an elementary exercise, designed to give you a fair chance of surviving Charon. You'll have to go through your whole repertory here: tools, weapons, maneuvers. And you'll find that, at these temperatures, tools don't work the way they should; weapons don't want to fire. And people move v-e-r-y cautiously."

He studied the clipboard in his hand. "Right now, you have forty-nine women and forty-eight men. Two deaths on Earth, one psychiatric release. Having read an outline of your training program, I'm frankly surprised that so many of you pulled through.

"But you might as well know that I won't be displeased if as few as fifty of you, half, graduate from this final phase. And the only way not to graduate is to die. Here. The only way anybody gets back to Earth—including me—is after a combat tour.

"You will complete your training in one month. From here you go to Stargate collapsar, half a light year away. You will stay at the settlement on Stargate 1, the largest portal planet, until replacements arrive. Hopefully, that will be no more than a month; another group is due here as soon as you leave.

"When you leave Stargate, you will go to some strategically important collapsar, set up a military base there, and fight the enemy, if attacked. Otherwise, you will maintain the base until further orders.

"The last two weeks of your training will consist of constructing exactly that kind of a base, on darkside. There you will be totally isolated from Miami Base: no communication, no medical evacuation, no resupply. Sometime before the two weeks are up, your defense facilities will be evaluated in an attack by guided drones. They will be armed."

They had spent all that money on us just to kill us in training?

"All of the permanent personnel here on Charon are combat veterans. Thus, all of us are forty to fifty years of age. But I think we can keep up with you. Two of us will be with you at all times and will accompany you at least as far as Stargate. They are Captain Sherman Stott, your company commander, and Sergeant Octavio Cortez, your first sergeant. Gentlemen?"

Two men in the front row stood easily and turned to face us. Captain Stott was a little smaller than the major, but cut from the same mold: face hard and smooth as porcelain, cynical half-smile, a precise centimeter of beard framing a large chin, looking thirty at the most. He wore a large, gunpowder-type pistol on his hip.

Sergeant Cortez was another story, a horror story. His head was shaved and the wrong shape, flattened out on one side, where

a large piece of skull had obviously been taken out. His face was
very dark and seamed with wrinkles and scars. Half his left ear
was missing, and his eyes were as expressive as buttons on a machine. He had a moustache-and-beard combination that looked
like a skinny white caterpillar taking a lap around his mouth. On
anybody else, his schoolboy smile might look pleasant, but he was
about the ugliest, meanest-looking creature I'd ever seen. Still, if
you didn't look at his head and considered the lower six feet or so,
he could have posed as the "after" advertisement for a body-
building spa. Neither Stott nor Cortez wore any ribbons. Cortez
had a small pocket-laser suspended in a magnetic rig, sideways,
under his left armpit. It had wooden grips that were worn smooth.

"Now, before I turn you over to the tender mercies of these
two gentlemen, let me caution you again:

"Two months ago there was not a living soul on this planet,
just some leftover equipment from the expedition of 1991. A
working force of forty-five men struggled for a month to erect this
base. Twenty-four of them, more than half, died in the construc-
tion of it. This is the most dangerous planet men have ever tried to
live on, but the places you'll be going will be this bad and worse.
Your cadre will try to keep you alive for the next month. Listen to
them . . . and follow their example; all of them have survived here
much longer than you'll have to. Captain?" The captain stood up
as the major went out the door.

"Tench-*hut!*" The last syllable was like an explosion and we
all jerked to our feet.

"Now I'm only gonna say this *once* so you better listen," he
growled. "We *are* in a combat situation here, and in a combat situation there is only *one* penalty for disobedience or insubordina-
tion." He jerked the pistol from his hip and held it by the barrel,
like a club. "This is an Army model 1911 automatic *pistol*, caliber
.45, and it is a primitive but effective weapon. The Sergeant and I
are authorized to use our weapons to kill to enforce discipline.
Don't make us do it because we will. We *will.*" He put the pistol
back. The holster snap made a loud crack in the dead quiet.

"Sergeant Cortez and I between us have killed more people
than are sitting in this room. Both of us fought in Vietnam on the
American side and both of us joined the United Nations Interna-
tional Guard more than ten years ago. I took a break in grade from
major for the privilege of commanding this company, and First
Sergeant Cortez took a break from sub-major, because we are

both *combat* soldiers and this is the first *combat* situation since 1987.

"Keep in mind what I've said while the First Sergeant instructs you more specifically in what your duties will be under this command. Take over, Sergeant." He turned on his heel and strode out of the room. The expression on his face hadn't changed one millimeter during the whole harangue.

The First Sergeant moved like a heavy machine with lots of ball bearings. When the door hissed shut, he swiveled ponderously to face us and said, "At ease, siddown," in a surprisingly gentle voice. He sat on a table in the front of the room. It creaked, but held.

"Now the captain talks scary and I look scary, but we both mean well. You'll be working pretty closely with me, so you better get used to this thing I've got hanging in front of my brain. You probably won't see the captain much, except on maneuvers."

He touched the flat part of his head. "And speaking of brains, I still have just about all of mine, in spite of Chinese efforts to the contrary. All of us old vets who mustered into UNEF had to pass the same criteria that got you drafted by the Elite Conscription Act. So I suspect all of you are smart and tough—but just keep in mind that the captain and I are smart and tough *and* experienced."

He flipped through the roster without really looking at it. "Now, as the captain said, there'll be only one kind of disciplinary action on maneuvers. Capital punishment. But normally *we* won't have to kill you for disobeying; Charon'll save us the trouble.

"Back in the billeting area, it'll be another story. We don't much care what you do inside. Grab ass all day and fuck all night, makes no difference. . . . But once you suit up and go outside, you've gotta have discipline that would shame a Centurian. There will be situations where one stupid act could kill us all.

"Anyhow, the first thing we've gotta do is get you fitted to your fighting suits. The armorer's waiting at your billet; he'll take you one at a time. Let's go."

"Now I know you got lectured back on Earth on what a fighting suit can do." The armorer was a small man, partially bald, with no insignia of rank on his coveralls. Sergeant Cortez had told us to call him "sir," since he was a lieutenant.

"But I'd like to reinforce a couple of points, maybe add some things your instructors Earthside weren't clear about or couldn't know. Your First Sergeant was kind enough to consent to being my visual aid. Sergeant?"

Cortez slipped out of his coveralls and came up to the little raised platform where a fighting suit was standing, popped open like a man-shaped clam. He backed into it and slipped his arms into the rigid sleeves. There was a click and the thing swung shut with a sigh. It was bright green with CORTEZ stenciled in white letters on the helmet.

"Camouflage, Sergeant." The green faded to white, then dirty gray. "This is good camouflage for Charon and most of your portal planets," said Cortez, as if from a deep well. "But there are several other combinations available." The gray dappled and brightened to a combination of greens and browns: "Jungle." Then smoothed out to a hard light ochre: "Desert." Dark brown, darker, to a deep flat black: "Night or space."

"Very good, Sergeant. To my knowledge, this is the only feature of the suit that was perfected after your training. The control is around your left wrist and is admittedly awkward. But once you find the right combination, it's easy to lock in.

"Now, you didn't get much in-suit training Earthside. We didn't want you to get used to using the thing in a friendly environment. The fighting suit is the deadliest personal weapon ever built, and with no weapon is it easier for the user to kill himself through carelessness. Turn around, Sergeant.

"Case in point." He tapped a large square protuberance between the shoulders. "Exhaust fins. As you know, the suit tries to keep you at a comfortable temperature no matter what the weather's like outside. The material of the suit is as near to a perfect insulator as we could get, consistent with mechanical demands. Therefore, these fins get *hot*—especially hot, compared to darkside temperatures—as they bleed off the body's heat.

"All you have to do is lean up against a boulder of frozen gas; there's lots of it around. The gas will sublime off faster than it can escape from the fins; in escaping, it will push against the surrounding 'ice' and fracture it . . . and in about one-hundredth of a second, you have the equivalent of a hand grenade going off right below your neck. You'll never feel a thing.

"Variations on this theme have killed eleven people in the past two months. And they were just building a bunch of huts.

"I assume you know how easily the waldo capabilities can kill you or your companions. Anybody want to shake hands with the sergeant?" He paused, then stepped over and clasped his glove. "He's had lots of practice. Until *you* have, be extremely careful. You might scratch an itch and wind up breaking your back. Remember, semi-logarithmic response: two pounds' pressure exerts five pounds' force; three pounds' gives ten; four pounds', twenty-three; five pounds', forty-seven. Most of you can muster up a grip of well over a hundred pounds. Theoretically, you could rip a steel girder in two with that, amplified. Actually, you'd destroy the material of your gloves and, at least on Charon, die very quickly. It'd be a race between decompression and flash-freezing. You'd die no matter which won.

"The leg waldos are also dangerous, even though the amplification is less extreme. Until you're really skilled, don't try to run, or jump. You're likely to trip, and that means you're likely to die.

"Charon's gravity is three-fourths of Earth normal, so it's not too bad. But on a really small world, like Luna, you could take a running jump and not come down for twenty minutes, just keep sailing over the horizon. Maybe bash into a mountain at eighty meters per second. On a small asteroid, it'd be no trick at all to run up to escape velocity and be off on an informal tour of intergalactic space. It's a slow way to travel.

"Tomorrow morning, we'll start teaching you how to stay alive inside this infernal machine. The rest of the afternoon and evening, I'll call you one at a time to be fitted. That's all, Sergeant."

Cortez went to the door and turned the stopcock that let air into the airlock. A bank of infrared lamps went on to keep air from freezing inside it. When the pressures were equalized, he shut the stopcock, unclamped the door and stepped in, clamping it shut behind him. A pump hummed for about a minute, evacuating the airlock; then he stepped out and sealed the outside door.

It was pretty much like the ones on Luna.

"First I want Private Omar Almizar. The rest of you can go find your bunks. I'll call you over the squawker."

"Alphabetical order, sir?"

"Yep. About ten minutes apiece. If your name begins with Z, you might as well get sacked."

That was Rogers. She probably was thinking about getting sacked.

The sun was a hard white point directly overhead. It was a lot brighter than I had expected it to be; since we were eighty AUs out, it was only one-6400th as bright as it is on Earth. Still, it was putting out about as much light as a powerful streetlamp.

"This is considerably more light than you'll have on a portal planet." Captain Stott's voice crackled in our collective ear. "Be glad that you'll be able to watch your step."

We were lined up, single-file, on the permaplast sidewalk that connected the billet and the supply hut. We'd practiced walking inside, all morning, and this wasn't any different except for the exotic scenery. Though the light was rather dim, you could see all the way to the horizon quite clearly, with no atmosphere in the way. A black cliff that looked too regular to be natural stretched from one horizon to the other, passing within a kilometer of us. The ground was obsidian-black, mottled with patches of white or bluish ice. Next to the supply hut was a small mountain of snow in a bin marked OXYGEN.

The suit was fairly comfortable, but it gave you the odd feeling of simultaneously being a marionette and a puppeteer. You apply the impulse to move your leg and the suit picks it up and magnifies it and moves your leg *for* you.

"Today we're only going to walk around the company area, and nobody will *leave* the company area." The captain wasn't wearing his .45—unless he carried it as a good luck charm, under his suit—but he had a laser-finger like the rest of us. And his was probably hooked up.

Keeping an interval of at least two meters between each person, we stepped off the permaplast and followed the captain over smooth rock. We walked carefully for about an hour, spiraling out, and finally stopped at the far edge of the perimeter.

"Now everybody pay close attention. I'm going out to that blue slab of ice"—it was a big one, about twenty meters away—"and show you something that you'd better know if you want to stay alive."

He walked out in a dozen confident steps. "First I have to heat up a rock—filters down." I squeezed the stud under my armpit and the filter slid into place over my image converter. The captain pointed his finger at a black rock the size of a basketball, and gave it a short burst. The glare rolled a long shadow of the captain over us and beyond. The rock shattered into a pile of hazy splinters.

"It doesn't take long for these to cool down." He stopped and picked up a piece. "This one is probably twenty or twenty-five degrees. Watch." He tossed the "warm" rock onto the ice slab. It skittered around in a crazy pattern and shot off the side. He tossed another one, and it did the same.

"As you know, you are not quite *perfectly* insulated. These rocks are about the temperature of the soles of your boots. If you try to stand on a slab of hydrogen, the same thing will happen to you. Except that the rock is *already* dead.

"The reason for this behavior is that the rock makes a slick interface with the ice—a little puddle of liquid hydrogen—and rides a few molecules above the liquid on a cushion of hydrogen vapor. This makes the rock or *you* a frictionless bearing as far as the ice is concerned, and you *can't* stand up without any friction under your boots.

"After you have lived in your suit for a month or so you *should* be able to survive falling down, but right *now* you just don't know enough. Watch."

The captain flexed and hopped up onto the slab. His feet shot out from under him and he twisted around in midair, landing on hands and knees. He slipped off and stood on the ground.

"The idea is to keep your exhaust fins from making contact with the frozen gas. Compared to the ice they are as hot as a blast furnace, and contact with any weight behind it will result in an explosion."

After that demonstration, we walked around for another hour or so and returned to the billet. Once through the airlock, we had to mill around for a while, letting the suits get up to something like room temperature. Somebody came up and touched helmets with me.

"William?" She had MCCOY stenciled above her faceplate.

"Hi, Sean. Anything special?"

"I just wondered if you had anyone to sleep with tonight."

That's right; I'd forgotten. There wasn't any sleeping roster here. Everybody chose his own partner. "Sure, I mean, uh, no . . . no, I haven't asked anybody. Sure, if you want to. . . ."

"Thanks, William. See you later." I watched her walk away and thought that if anybody could make a fighting suit look sexy, it'd be Sean. But even she couldn't.

Cortez decided we were warm enough and led us to the suit room, where we backed the things into place and hooked them up to the charging plates. (Each suit had a little chunk of plutonium that would power it for several years, but we were supposed to run on fuel cells as much as possible.) After a lot of shuffling around, everybody finally got plugged in and we were allowed to unsuit— ninety-seven naked chickens squirming out of bright green eggs. It was *cold*—the air, the floor and especially the suits—and we made a pretty disorderly exit toward the lockers.

I slipped on tunic, trousers and sandals and was still cold. I took my cup and joined the line for soya. Everybody was jumping up and down to keep warm.

"How c-cold, do you think, it is, M-Mandella?" That was McCoy.

"I don't, even want, to think, about it." I stopped jumping and rubbed myself as briskly as possible, while holding a cup in one hand. "At least as cold as Missouri was."

"Ung . . . wish they'd, get some, fucken, heat in, this place." It always affects the small women more than anybody else. McCoy was the littlest one in the company, a waspwaist doll barely five feet high.

"They've got the airco going. It can't be long now."

"I wish I, was a big, slab of, meat like, you."

I was glad she wasn't.

We had our first casualty on the third day, learning how to dig holes.

With such large amounts of energy stored in a soldier's weapons, it wouldn't be practical for him to hack out a hole in the frozen ground with the conventional pick and shovel. Still, you can launch grenades all day and get nothing but shallow depressions—so the usual method is to bore a hole in the ground with the hand laser, drop a timed charge in after it's cooled down and, ideally, fill the hole with stuff. Of course, there's not much loose rock on Charon, unless you've already blown a hole nearby.

The only difficult thing about the procedure is in getting away. To be safe, we were told, you've got to either be behind something really solid, or be at least a hundred meters away. You've got about three minutes after setting the charge, but you can't just sprint away. Not safely, not on Charon.

The accident happened when we were making a really deep hole, the kind you want for a large underground bunker. For this, we had to blow a hole, then climb down to the bottom of the crater and repeat the procedure again and again until the hole was deep enough. Inside the crater we used charges with a five-minute delay, but it hardly seemed enough time—you really had to go it slow, picking your way up the crater's edge.

Just about everybody had blown a double hole; everybody but me and three others. I guess we were the only ones paying really close attention when Bovanovitch got into trouble. All of us were a good two hundred meters away. With my image converter turned up to about forty power, I watched her disappear over the rim of the crater. After that, I could only listen in on her conversation with Cortez.

"I'm on the bottom, Sergeant." Normal radio procedure was suspended for maneuvers like this; nobody but the trainee and Cortez was allowed to broadcast.

"Okay, move to the center and clear out the rubble. Take your time. No rush until you pull the pin."

"Sure, Sergeant." We could hear small echoes of rocks clattering, sound conduction through her boots. She didn't say anything for several minutes.

"Found bottom." She sounded a little out of breath.

"Ice or rock?"

"Oh, it's rock, Sergeant. The greenish stuff."

"Use a low setting, then. One point two, dispersion four."

"God darn it, Sergeant, that'll take forever."

"Yeah, but that stuff's got hydrated crystals in it—heat it up too fast and you might make it fracture. And we'd just have to leave you there, girl. Dead and bloody."

"Okay, one point two dee four." The inside edge of the crater flickered red with reflected laser light.

"When you get about half a meter deep, squeeze it up to dee two."

"Roger." It took her exactly seventeen minutes, three of them at dispersion two. I could imagine how tired her shooting arm was.

"Now rest for a few minutes. When the bottom of the hole stops glowing, arm the charge and drop it in. Then *walk* out, understand? You'll have plenty of time."

"I understand, Sergeant. Walk out." She sounded nervous. Well, you don't often have to tiptoe away from a twenty-microton tachyon bomb. We listened to her breathing for a few minutes.

"Here goes." Faint slithering sound, the bomb sliding down.

"Slow and easy now. You've got five minutes."

"Y-yeah. Five." Her footsteps started out slow and regular. Then, after she started climbing the side, the sounds were less regular, maybe a little frantic. And with four minutes to go—

"Shit!" A loud scraping noise, then clatters and bumps. "Shit-shit."

"What's wrong, private?"

"Oh, shit." Silence. "Shit!"

"Private, you don't wanna get shot, you *tell me what's wrong!*"

"I . . . shit, I'm stuck. Fucken rockslide . . . shit. . . . DO SOMETHING! I can't move, shit I can't move I, I—"

"Shut up! How deep?"

"Can't move my, shit, my fucken legs. HELP ME—"

"Then goddammit use your arms—push! You can move a ton with each hand." Three minutes.

She stopped cussing and started to mumble, in Russian, I guess, a low monotone. She was panting, and you could hear rocks tumbling away.

"I'm free." Two minutes.

"Go as fast as you can." Cortez's voice was flat, emotionless.

At ninety seconds she appeared, crawling over the rim. "Run, girl. . . . You better run." She ran five or six steps and fell, skidded a few meters and got back up, running; fell again, got up again—

It looked as though she was going pretty fast, but she had only covered about thirty meters when Cortez said, "All right, Bovanovitch, get down on your stomach and lie still." Ten seconds, but she didn't hear or she wanted to get just a little more distance, and she kept running, careless leaping strides, and at the high point of one leap there was a flash and a rumble, and something big hit her below the neck, and her headless body spun off end over end through space, trailing a red-black spiral of flash-frozen blood that settled gracefully to the ground, a path of crystal powder that nobody disturbed while we gathered rocks to cover the juiceless thing at the end of it.

That night Cortez didn't lecture us, didn't even show up for night-chop. We were all very polite to each other and nobody was afraid to talk about it.

I sacked with Rogers—everybody sacked with a good friend—but all she wanted to do was cry, and she cried so long and so hard that she got me doing it, too.

"Fire team *A*—move out!" The twelve of us advanced in a ragged line toward the simulated bunker. It was about a kilometer away, across a carefully prepared obstacle course. We could move pretty fast, since all of the ice had been cleared from the field, but even with ten days' experience we weren't ready to do more than an easy jog.

I carried a grenade launcher loaded with tenth-microton practice grenades. Everybody had their laser-fingers set at a point oh eight dee one, not much more than a flashlight. This was a *simulated* attack—the bunker and its robot defender cost too much to use once and be thrown away.

"Team *B*, follow. Team leaders, take over."

We approached a clump of boulders at about the halfway mark, and Potter, my team leader, said, "Stop and cover." We clustered behind the rocks and waited for Team *B*.

Barely visible in their blackened suits, the dozen men and women whispered by us. As soon as they were clear, they jogged left, out of our line of sight.

"Fire!" Red circles of light danced a half-klick downrange, where the bunker was just visible. Five hundred meters was the limit for these practice grenades; but I might luck out, so I lined the launcher up on the image of the bunker, held it at a forty-five degree angle and popped off a salvo of three.

Return fire from the bunker started before my grenades even landed. Its automatic lasers were no more powerful than the ones we were using, but a direct hit would deactivate your image converter, leaving you blind. It was setting down a random field of fire, not even coming close to the boulders we were hiding behind.

Three magnesium-bright flashes blinked simultaneously about thirty meters short of the bunker. "Mandella! I thought you were supposed to be good with that thing."

"Damn it, Potter—it only throws half a klick. Once we get closer, I'll lay 'em right on top, every time."

"Sure you will." I didn't say anything. She wouldn't be team leader forever. Besides, she hadn't been such a bad girl before the power went to her head.

Since the grenadier is the assistant team leader, I was slaved into Potter's radio and could hear B team talk to her.

"Potter, this is Freeman. Losses?"

"Potter here—no, looks like they were concentrating on you."

"Yeah, we lost three. Right now we're in a depression about eighty, a hundred meters down from you. We can give cover whenever you're ready."

"Okay, start." Soft click: "A team, follow me." She slid out from behind the rock and turned on the faint pink beacon beneath her powerpack. I turned on mine and moved out to run alongside of her, and the rest of the team fanned out in a trailing wedge. Nobody fired while A team laid down a cover for us.

All I could hear was Potter's breathing and the soft crunch-crunch of my boots. Couldn't see much of anything, so I tongued the image converter up to a log two intensification. That made the image kind of blurry but adequately bright. Looked like the bunker had B team pretty well pinned down; they were getting quite a roasting. All of their return fire was laser. They must have lost their grenadier.

"Potter, this is Mandella. Shouldn't we take some of the heat off B team?"

"Soon as I can find us good enough cover. Is that all right with you? Private?" She'd been promoted to corporal for the duration of the exercise.

We angled to the right and lay down behind a slab of rock. Most of the others found cover nearby, but a few had to hug the ground.

"Freeman, this is Potter."

"Potter, this is Smithy. Freeman's out; Samuels is out. We only have five men left. Give us some cover so we can get—"

"Roger, Smithy." Click. "Open up, A team. The B's are really hurtin'."

I peeked out over the edge of the rock. My rangefinder said that the bunker was about three hundred fifty meters away, still pretty far. I aimed a smidgeon high and popped three, then down a couple of degrees, three more. The first ones overshot by about twenty meters; then the second salvo flared up directly in front of the bunker. I tried to hold on that angle and popped fifteen, the rest of the magazine, in the same direction.

I should have ducked down behind the rock to reload, but I wanted to see where the fifteen would land, so I kept my eyes on the bunker while I reached back to unclip another magazine—

When the laser hit my image converter, there was a red glare so intense it seemed to go right through my eyes and bounce off the back of my skull. It must have been only a few milliseconds before the converter overloaded and went blind, but the bright green afterimage hurt my eyes for several minutes.

Since I was officially "dead," my radio automatically cut off, and I had to remain where I was until the mock battle was over. With no sensory input besides the feel of my own skin (and it ached where the image converter had shone on it) and the ringing in my ears, it seemed like an awfully long time. Finally, a helmet clanked against mine.

"You okay, Mandella?" Potter's voice.

"Sorry, I died of boredom twenty minutes ago."

"Stand up and take my hand." I did so and we shuffled back to the billet. It must have taken over an hour. She didn't say anything more, all the way back—it's a pretty awkward way to communicate—but after we'd cycled through the airlock and warmed up, she helped me undo my suit. I got ready for a mild tongue-lashing, but when the suit popped open, before I could even get my eyes adjusted to the light, she grabbed me around the neck and planted a wet kiss on my mouth.

"Nice shooting, Mandella."

"Huh?"

"Didn't you see? Of course not. . . . The last salvo before you got hit—four direct hits. The bunker decided it was knocked out, and all we had to do was walk the rest of the way."

"Great." I scratched my face under the eyes, and some dry skin flaked off. She giggled.

"You should see yourself. You look like—"

"All personnel, report to the assembly area." That was the captain's voice. Bad news, usually.

She handed me a tunic and sandals. "Let's go." The assembly

area-chop hall was just down the corridor. There was a row of roll-call buttons at the door; I pressed the one beside my name. Four of the names were covered with black tape. That was good, only four. We hadn't lost anybody during today's maneuvers.

The captain was sitting on the raised dais, which at least meant we didn't have to go through the tench-hut bullshit. The place filled up in less than a minute; a soft chime indicated the roll was complete.

Captain Stott didn't stand up. "You did *fairly* well today. Nobody killed, and I expected some to be. In that respect you exceeded my expectations but in *every* other respect you did a poor job.

"I am glad you're taking good care of yourselves, because each of you represents an investment of over a million dollars and one-fourth of a human life.

"But in this simulated battle against a *very* stupid robot enemy, thirty-seven of you managed to walk into laser fire and be killed in a *sim*ulated way, and since dead people require no food *you* will require no food, for the next three days. Each person who was a casualty in this battle will be allowed only two liters of water and a vitamin ration each day."

We knew enough not to groan or anything, but there were some pretty disgusted looks, especially on the faces that had singed eyebrows and a pink rectangle of sunburn framing their eyes.

"Mandella."

"Sir?"

"You are far and away the worst-burned casualty. Was your image converter set on normal?"

Oh, shit. "No, sir. Log two."

"I see. Who was your team leader for the exercises?"

"Acting Corporal Potter, sir."

"Private Potter, did you order him to use image intensification?"

"Sir, I . . . I don't remember."

"You don't. Well, as a memory exercise you may join the dead people. Is that satisfactory?"

"Yes, sir."

"Good. Dead people get one last meal tonight and go on no rations starting tomorrow. Are there any questions?" He must have been kidding. "All right. Dismissed."

I selected the meal that looked as if it had the most calories and took my tray over to sit by Potter.

"That was a quixotic damn thing to do. But thanks."

"Nothing. I've been wanting to lose a few pounds anyway." I couldn't see where she was carrying any extra.

"I know a good exercise," I said. She smiled without looking up from her tray. "Have anybody for tonight?"

"Kind of thought I'd ask Jeff. . . ."

"Better hurry, then. He's lusting after Maejima." Well, that was mostly true. Everybody did.

"I don't know. Maybe we ought to save our strength. That third day . . ."

"Come on." I scratched the back of her hand lightly with a fingernail. "We haven't sacked since Missouri. Maybe I've learned something new."

"Maybe you have." She tilted her head up at me in a sly way. "Okay."

Actually, she was the one with the new trick. The French corkscrew, she called it. She wouldn't tell me who taught it to her though. I'd like to shake his hand. Once I got my strength back.

The two weeks' training around Miami Base eventually cost us eleven lives. Twelve, if you count Dahlquist. I guess having to spend the rest of your life on Charon with a hand and both legs missing is close enough to dying.

Foster was crushed in a landslide and Freeland had a suit malfunction that froze him solid before we could carry him inside. Most of the other deaders were people I didn't know all that well. But they all hurt. And they seemed to make us more scared rather than more cautious.

Now darkside. A flyer brought us over in groups of twenty and set us down beside a pile of building materials thoughtfully immersed in a pool of helium II.

We used grapples to haul the stuff out of the pool. It's not safe to go wading, since the stuff crawls all over you and it's hard to tell what's underneath; you could walk out onto a slab of hydrogen and be out of luck.

I'd suggested that we try to boil away the pool with our lasers, but ten minutes of concentrated fire didn't drop the helium level appreciably. It didn't boil, either; helium II is a "superfluid," so what evaporation there was had to take place evenly, all over the surface. No hot spots, so no bubbling.

We weren't supposed to use lights, to "avoid detection." There was plenty of starlight with your image converter cranked up to log three or four, but each stage of amplification meant some loss of detail. By log four the landscape looked like a crude monochrome painting, and you couldn't read the names on people's helmets unless they were right in front of you.

The landscape wasn't all that interesting, anyhow. There were half a dozen medium-sized meteor craters (all with exactly the same level of helium II in them) and the suggestion of some puny mountains just over the horizon. The uneven ground was the consistency of frozen spiderwebs; every time you put your foot down, you'd sink half an inch with a squeaking crunch. It could get on your nerves.

It took most of a day to pull all the stuff out of the pool. We took shifts napping, which you could do either standing up, sitting or lying on your stomach. I didn't do well in any of those positions, so I was anxious to get the bunker built and pressurized.

We couldn't build the thing underground—it'd just fill up with helium II—so the first thing to do was to build an insulating platform, a permaplast-vacuum sandwich three layers thick.

I was an acting corporal, with a crew of ten people. We were carrying the permaplast layers to the building site—two people can carry one easily—when one of "my" men slipped and fell on his back.

"Damn it, Singer, watch your step." We'd had a couple of deaders that way.

"Sorry, Corporal. I'm bushed. Just got my feet tangled up."

"Yeah, just watch it." He got back up all right, and he and his partner placed the sheet and went back to get another.

I kept my eye on Singer. In a few minutes he was practically staggering, not easy to do in that suit of cybernetic armor.

"Singer! After you set the plank, I want to see you."

"OK." He labored through the task and mooched over.

"Let me check your readout." I opened the door on his chest to expose the medical monitor. His temperature was two degrees high; blood pressure and heart rate both elevated. Not up to the red line, though.

"You sick or something?"

"Hell, Mandella, I feel OK, just tired. Since I fell I been a little dizzy."

I chinned the medic's combination. "Doc, this is Mandella. You wanna come over here for a minute?"

"Sure, where are you?" I waved and he walked over from poolside.

"What's the problem?" I showed him Singer's readout.

He knew what all the other little dials and things meant, so it took him a while. "As far as I can tell, Mandella . . . he's just hot."

"Hell, I coulda told you that," said Singer.

"Maybe you better have the armorer take a look at his suit."
We had two people who'd taken a crash course in suit maintenance; they were our "armorers."

I chinned Sanchez and asked him to come over with his tool kit.

"Be a couple of minutes, Corporal. Carryin' a plank."

"Well, put it down and get on over here." I was getting an un-
easy feeling. Waiting for him, the medic and I looked over
Singer's suit.

"Uh-oh," Doc Jones said. "Look at this." I went around to the
back and looked where he was pointing. Two of the fins on the
heat exchanger were bent out of shape.

"What's wrong?" Singer asked.

"You fell on your heat exchanger, right?"

"Sure, Corporal—that's it. It must not be working right."

"I don't think it's working at *all*," said Doc.

Sanchez came over with his diagnostic kit and we told him
what had happened. He looked at the heat exchanger, then
plugged a couple of jacks into it and got a digital readout from a
little monitor in his kit. I didn't know what it was measuring, but it
came out zero to eight decimal places.

Heard a soft click, Sanchez chinning my private frequency.
"Corporal, this guy's a deader."

"What? Can't you fix the goddamn thing?"

"Maybe . . . maybe I could, if I could take it apart. But there's
no way—"

"Hey! Sanchez?" Singer was talking on the general freak.
"Find out what's wrong?" He was panting.

Click. "Keep your pants on, man, we're working on it." *Click.*
"He won't last long enough for us to get the bunker pressurized.
And I can't work on the heat exchanger from outside of the suit."

"You've got a spare suit, haven't you?"

"Two of 'em, the fit-anybody kind. But there's no place . . .
say . . ."

"Right. Go get one of the suits warmed up." I chinned the general freak. "Listen, Singer, we've gotta get you out of that thing.
Sanchez has a spare suit, but to make the switch, we're gonna have
to build a house around you. Understand?"

"Huh-uh."

"Look, we'll make a box with you inside, and hook it up to the
life-support unit. That way you can breathe while you make the
switch."

"Soun's pretty compis . . . compil . . . cated t'me."

"Look, just come along—"

"I'll be all right, man, jus' lemme res'. . . ."

I grabbed his arm and led him to the building site. He was really weaving. Doc took his other arm, and between us, we kept him from falling over.

"Corporal Ho, this is Corporal Mandella." Ho was in charge of the life-support unit.

"Go away, Mandella, I'm, busy."

"You're going to be busier." I outlined the problem to her. While her group hurried to adapt the LSU—for this purpose, it need only be an air hose and heater—I got my crew to bring around six slabs of permaplast, so we could build a big box around Singer and the extra suit. It would look like a huge coffin, a meter square and six meters long.

We set the suit down on the slab that would be the floor of the coffin. "OK, Singer, let's go."

No answer.

"Singer, let's go."

No answer.

"Singer!" He was just standing there. Doc Jones checked his readout.

"He's out, man, unconscious."

My mind raced. There might just be room for another person in the box. "Give me a hand here." I took Singer's shoulders and Doc took his feet, and we carefully laid him out at the feet of the empty suit.

Then I lay down myself, above the suit. "OK, close'er up."

"Look, Mandella, if anybody goes in there, it oughta be me."

"Fuck you, Doc. *My* job. My man." That sounded all wrong. William Mandella, boy hero.

They stood a slab up on edge—it had two openings for the LSU input and exhaust—and proceeded to weld it to the bottom plank with a narrow laser beam. On Earth, we'd just use glue, but here the only fluid was helium, which has lots of interesting properties, but is definitely not sticky.

After about ten minutes we were completely walled up. I could feel the LSU humming. I switched on my suit light—the first time since we landed on darkside—and the glare made purple blotches dance in front of my eyes.

"Mandella, this is Ho. Stay in your suit at least two or three minutes. We're putting hot air in, but it's coming back just this side of liquid." I watched the purple fade for a while.

"OK, it's still cold, but you can make it." I popped my suit. It wouldn't open all the way, but I didn't have too much trouble getting out. The suit was still cold enough to take some skin off my fingers and butt as I wiggled out.

I had to crawl feet-first down the coffin to get to Singer. It got darker fast, moving away from my light. When I popped his suit a rush of hot stink hit me in the face. In the dim light his skin was dark red and splotchy. His breathing was very shallow and I could see his heart palpitating.

First I unhooked the relief tubes—an unpleasant business— then the biosensors; and then I had the problem of getting his arms out of their sleeves.

It's pretty easy to do for yourself. You twist this way and turn that way and the arm pops out. Doing it from the outside is a different matter: I had to twist his arm and then reach under and move the suit's arm to match—it takes muscle to move a suit around from the outside.

Once I had one arm out it was pretty easy; I just crawled forward, putting my feet on the suit's shoulders, and pulled on his free arm. He slid out of the suit like an oyster slipping out of its shell.

I popped the spare suit and after a lot of pulling and pushing, managed to get his legs in. Hooked up the biosensors and the front relief tube. He'd have to do the other one himself; it's too complicated. For the nth time I was glad not to have been born female; they have to have two of those damned plumber's friends, instead of just one and a simple hose.

I left his arms out of the sleeves. The suit would be useless for any kind of work, anyhow; waldos have to be tailored to the individual.

His eyelids fluttered. "Man . . . della. Where . . . the fuck . . ."

I explained, slowly, and he seemed to get most of it. "Now I'm gonna close you up and go get into my suit. I'll have the crew cut the end off this thing and I'll haul you out. Got it?"

He nodded. Strange to see that—when you nod or shrug inside a suit, it doesn't communicate anything.

I crawled into my suit, hooked up the attachments and chinned the general freak. "Doc, I think he's gonna be OK. Get us out of here now."

"Will do." Ho's voice. The LSU hum was replaced by a chatter, then a throb. Evacuating the box to prevent an explosion.

One corner of the seam grew red, then white, and a bright

crimson beam lanced through, not a foot away from my head. I scrunched back as far as I could. The beam slid up the seam and around three corners, back to where it started. The end of the box fell away slowly, trailing filaments of melted 'plast.

"Wait for the stuff to harden, Mandella."

"Sanchez, I'm not that stupid."

"Here you go." Somebody tossed a line to me. That *would* be smarter than dragging him out by myself. I threaded a long bight under his arms and tied it behind his neck. Then I scrambled out to help them pull, which was silly—they had a dozen people already lined up to haul.

Singer got out all right and was actually sitting up while Doc Jones checked his readout. People were asking me about it and congratulating me, when suddenly Ho said "Look!" and pointed toward the horizon.

It was a black ship, coming in fast. I just had time to think it wasn't fair, they weren't supposed to attack until the last few days, and then the ship was right on top of us.

We all flopped to the ground instinctively, but the ship didn't attack. It blasted braking rockets and dropped to land on skids. Then it skied around to come to a rest beside the building site.

Everybody had it figured out and was standing around sheepishly when the two suited figures stepped out of the ship.

A familiar voice crackled over the general freak. "Every *one* of you saw us coming in and not *one* of you responded with laser fire. It wouldn't have done any good but it would have indicated a certain amount of fighting spirit. You have a week or less before the real thing and since the sergeant and *I* will be here *I* will insist that you show a little more will to live. Acting Sergeant Potter."

"Here, sir."

"Get me a detail of twelve people to unload cargo. We brought a hundred small robot drones for *target* practice so that you might have at least a fighting chance when a live target comes over.

"Move *now*. We only have thirty minutes before the ship returns to Miami."

I checked, and it was actually more like forty minutes.

Having the captain and sergeant there didn't really make much difference. We were still on our own; they were just observing.

Once we got the floor down, it only took one day to complete the bunker. It was a gray oblong, featureless except for the airlock blister and four windows. On top was a swivel-mounted gigawatt laser. The operator—you couldn't call him a "gunner"—sat in a chair holding dead-man switches in both hands. The laser wouldn't fire as long as he was holding one of those switches. If he let go, it would automatically aim for any moving aerial object and fire at will. Primary detection and aiming was by means of a kilometer-high antenna mounted beside the bunker.

It was the only arrangement that could really be expected to work, with the horizon so close and human reflexes so slow. You couldn't have the thing fully automatic, because in theory, friendly ships might also approach.

The aiming computer could choose among up to twelve targets appearing simultaneously (firing at the largest ones first). And it would get all twelve in the space of half a second.

The installation was partly protected from enemy fire by an efficient ablative layer that covered everything except the human operator. But then, they *were* dead-man switches. One man above guarding eighty inside. The army's good at that kind of arithmetic.

Once the bunker was finished, half of us stayed inside at all times—feeling very much like targets—taking turns operating the laser, while the other half went on maneuvers.

About four klicks from the base was a large "lake" of frozen hydrogen; one of our most important maneuvers was to learn how to get around on the treacherous stuff.

It wasn't too difficult. You couldn't stand up on it, so you had to belly down and sled.

If you had somebody to push you from the edge, getting started was no problem. Otherwise, you had to scrabble with your hands and feet, pushing down as hard as was practical, until you started moving, in a series of little jumps. Once started, you'd keep going until you ran out of ice. You could steer a little bit by digging in, hand and foot, on the appropriate side, but you couldn't slow to a stop that way. So it was a good idea not to go too fast and wind up positioned in such a way that your helmet didn't absorb the shock of stopping.

We went through all the things we'd done on the Miami side: weapons practice, demolition, attack patterns. We also launched drones at irregular intervals, toward the bunker. Thus, ten or fifteen times a day, the operators got to demonstrate their skill in letting go of the handles as soon as the proximity light went on.

I had four hours of that, like everybody else. I was nervous until the first "attack," when I saw how little there was to it. The light went on, I let go, the gun aimed, and when the drone peeped over the horizon—*zzt!* Nice touch of color, the molten metal spraying through space. Otherwise not too exciting.

So none of us were worried about the upcoming "graduation exercise," thinking it would be just more of the same.

Miami Base attacked on the thirteenth day with two simultaneous missiles streaking over opposite sides of the horizon at some forty kilometers per second. The laser vaporized the first one with no trouble, but the second got within eight klicks of the bunker before it was hit.

We were coming back from maneuvers, about a klick away from the bunker. I wouldn't have seen it happen if I hadn't been looking directly at the bunker the moment of the attack.

The second missile sent a shower of molten debris straight toward the bunker. Eleven pieces hit, and, as we later reconstructed it, this is what happened:

The first casualty was Maejima, so well-loved Maejima, inside the bunker, who was hit in the back and the head and died instantly. With the drop in pressure, the LSU went into high gear. Friedman was standing in front of the main airco outlet and was blown into the opposite wall hard enough to knock him unconscious; he died of decompression before the others could get him to his suit.

Everybody else managed to stagger through the gale and get into their suits, but Garcia's suit had been holed and didn't do him any good.

By the time we got there, they had turned off the LSU and were welding up the holes in the wall. One man was trying to scrape up the unrecognizable mess that had been Maejima. I could hear him sobbing and retching. They had already taken Garcia and Friedman outside for burial. The captain took over the repair detail from Potter. Sergeant Cortez led the sobbing man over to a corner and came back to work on cleaning up Maejima's remains, alone. He didn't order anybody to help and nobody volunteered.

As a graduation exercise, we were unceremoniously stuffed into a ship—*Earth's Hope*, the same one we rode to Charon—and bundled off to Stargate at a little more than one gee.

The trip seemed endless, about six months subjective time, and boring, but not as hard on the carcass as going to Charon had been. Captain Stott made us review our training orally, day by day, and we did exercises every day until we were worn to a collective frazzle.

Stargate 1 was like Charon's darkside, only more so. The base on Stargate 1 was smaller than Miami Base—only a little bigger than the one we constructed on darkside—and we were due to lay over a week to help expand the facilities. The crew there was very glad to see us, especially the two females, who looked a little worn around the edges.

We all crowded into the small dining hall, where Submajor Williamson, the man in charge of Stargate 1, gave us some disconcerting news:

"Everybody get comfortable. Get off the tables, though, there's plenty of floor.

"I have some idea of what you just went through, training on Charon. I won't say it's all been wasted. But where you're headed, things will be quite different. Warmer."

He paused to let that soak in.

"Aleph Aurigae, the first collapsar ever detected, revolves around the normal star Epsilon Aurigae in a twenty-seven year orbit. The enemy has a base of operations, not on a regular portal planet of Aleph, but on a planet in orbit around Epsilon. We don't know much about the planet, just that it goes around Epsilon once every 745 days, is about three-fourths the size of Earth, and has an albedo of 0.8, meaning it's probably covered with clouds. We can't say precisely how hot it will be, but judging from its distance from Epsilon, it's probably rather hotter than Earth. Of course, we don't know whether you'll be working . . . fighting on lightside or darkside, equator or poles. It's highly unlikely that the atmosphere will be breathable—at any rate, you'll stay inside your suits.

"Now you know exactly as much about where you're going as I do. Questions?"

"Sir," Stein drawled, "now we know where we're goin' . . . anybody know what we're goin' to do when we get there?"

Williamson shrugged. "That's up to your captain—and your sergeant, and the captain of *Earth's Hope*, and *Hope*'s logistic computer. We just don't have enough data yet to project a course of action for you. It may be a long and bloody battle; it may be just a case of walking in to pick up the pieces. Conceivably, the Taurans might want to make a peace offer"—Cortez snorted—"in which case you would simply be part of our muscle, our bargaining power." He looked at Cortez mildly. "No one can say for sure."

The orgy that night was amusing, but it was like trying to sleep in the middle of a raucous beach party. The only area big enough to sleep all of us was the dining hall; they draped a few bedsheets here and there for privacy, then unleashed Stargate's eighteen sex-starved men on our women, compliant and promiscuous by military custom (and law), but desiring nothing so much as sleep on solid ground.

The eighteen men acted as if they were compelled to try as many permutations as possible, and their performance was impressive (in a strictly quantitative sense, that is). Those of us who were keeping count led a cheering section for some of the more gifted members. I think that's the right word.

The next morning—and every other morning we were on Stargate 1—we staggered out of bed and into our suits, to go outside and work on the "new wing." Eventually, Stargate would be tactical and logistic headquarters for the war, with thousands of permanent personnel, guarded by half-a-dozen heavy cruisers in *Hope*'s class. When we started, it was two shacks and twenty people; when we left, it was four shacks and twenty people. The work was hardly work at all, compared to darkside, since we had plenty of light and got sixteen hours inside for every eight hours' work. And no drone attack for a final exam.

When we shuttled back up to the *Hope*, nobody was too happy about leaving (though some of the more popular females declared it'd be good to get some rest). Stargate was the last easy, safe assignment we'd have before taking up arms against the Taurans. And as Williamson had pointed out the first day, there was no way of predicting what *that* would be like.

Most of us didn't feel too enthusiastic about making a collapsar jump, either. We'd been assured that we wouldn't even feel it happen, just free fall all the way.

I wasn't convinced. As a physics student, I'd had the usual courses in general relativity and theories of gravitation. We only had a little direct data at that time—Stargate was discovered when I was in grade school—but the mathematical model seemed clear enough.

The collapsar Stargate was a perfect sphere about three kilometers in radius. It was suspended forever in a state of gravitational collapse that should have meant its surface was dropping toward its center at nearly the speed of light. Relativity propped it up, at least gave it the illusion of being there . . . the way all reality becomes illusory and observer-oriented when you study general relativity. Or Buddhism. Or get drafted.

At any rate, there would be a theoretical point in space-time when one end of our ship was just above the surface of the collapsar, and the other end was a kilometer away (in our frame of reference). In any sane universe, this would set up tidal stresses and tear the ship apart, and we would be just another million kilograms of degenerate matter on the theoretical surface, rushing headlong to nowhere for the rest of eternity or dropping to the center in the next trillionth of a second. You pays your money and you takes your frame of reference.

But they were right. We blasted away from Stargate 1, made a few course corrections and then just dropped, for about an hour.

Then a bell rang and we sank into our cushions under a steady two gravities of deceleration. We were in enemy territory.

We'd been decelerating at two gravities for almost nine days when the battle began. Lying on our couches being miserable, all we felt were two soft bumps, missiles being released. Some eight hours later, the squawkbox crackled: "Attention, all crew. This is the captain." Quinsana, the pilot, was only a lieutenant, but was allowed to call himself captain aboard the vessel, where he outranked all of us, even Captain Stott. "You grunts in the cargo hold can listen, too.

"We just engaged the enemy with two fifty-gigaton tachyon missiles and have destroyed both the enemy vessel and another object which it had launched approximately three microseconds before.

"The enemy has been trying to overtake us for the past 179 hours, ship time. At the time of the engagement, the enemy was moving at a little over half the speed of light, relative to Aleph, and was only about thirty AU's from *Earth's Hope*. It was moving at .47c relative to us, and thus we would have been coincident in space-time"—rammed!—"in a little more than nine hours. The missiles were launched at 0719 ship's time, and destroyed the enemy at 1540, both tachyon bombs detonating within a thousand klicks of the enemy objects."

The two missiles were a type whose propulsion system was itself only a barely-controlled tachyon bomb. They accelerated at a constant rate of 100 gees, and were traveling at a relativistic speed by the time the nearby mass of the enemy ship detonated them.

"We expect no further interference from enemy vessels. Our velocity with respect to Aleph will be zero in another five hours;

we will then begin the journey back. The return will take twenty-seven days." General moans and dejected cussing. Everybody knew all that already, of course; but we didn't care to be reminded of it.

So after another month of logy calisthenics and drill, at a constant two gravities, we got our first look at the planet we were going to attack. Invaders from outer space, yes sir.

It was a blinding white crescent waiting for us two AU's out from Epsilon. The captain had pinned down the location of the enemy base from fifty AU's out, and we had jockeyed in on a wide arc, keeping the bulk of the planet between them and us. That didn't mean we were sneaking up on them—quite the contrary; they launched three abortive attacks—but it put us in a stronger defensive position. Until we had to go to the surface, that is. Then only the ship and its Star Fleet crew would be reasonably safe.

Since the planet rotated rather slowly—once every ten and one-half days—a "stationary" orbit for the ship had to be 150,000 klicks out. This made the people in the ship feel quite secure, with 6,000 miles of rock and 90,000 miles of space between them and the enemy. But it meant a whole second's time lag in communication between us on the ground and the ship's battle computer. A person could get awful dead while that neutrino pulse crawled up and back.

Our vague orders were to attack the base and gain control, while damaging a minimum of enemy equipment. We were to take at least one enemy alive. We were under no circumstances to allow ourselves to be taken alive, however. And the decision wasn't up to us; one special pulse from the battle computer, and that speck of plutonium in your power plant would fiss with all of .01% efficiency, and you'd be nothing but a rapidly expanding, very hot plasma.

They strapped us into six scoutships—one platoon of twelve people in each—and we blasted away from *Earth's Hope* at eight gees. Each scoutship was supposed to follow its own carefully random path to our rendezvous point, 108 klicks from the base. Fourteen drone ships were launched at the same time, to confound the enemy's anti-spacecraft system.

The landing went off almost perfectly. One ship suffered minor damage, a near miss boiling away some of the ablative material on one side of the hull, but it'd still be able to make it and return, keeping its speed down while in the atmosphere.

We zigged and zagged and wound up first ship at the rendezvous point. There was only one trouble. It was under four kilometers of water.

I could almost hear that machine, 90,000 miles away, grinding its mental gears, adding this new bit of data. We proceeded just as if we were landing on solid ground: braking rockets, falling, skids out, hit the water, skip, hit the water, skip, hit the water, sink.

It would have made sense to go ahead and land on the bottom—we were streamlined, after all, and water just another fluid—but the hull wasn't strong enough to hold up a four-kilometer column of water. Sergeant Cortez was in the scoutship with us.

"Sarge, tell that computer to *do* something! We're gonna get—"

"Oh, shut up, Mandella. Trust in th' lord." "Lord" was definitely lower-case when Cortez said it.

There was a loud bubbly sigh, then another, and a slight increase in pressure on my back that meant the ship was rising. "Flotation bags?" Cortez didn't deign to answer, or didn't know.

That was it. We rose to within ten or fifteen meters of the surface and stopped, suspended there. Through the port I could see the surface above, shimmering like a mirror of hammered silver. I wondered what it would be like to be a fish and have a definite roof over your world.

I watched another ship splash in. It made a great cloud of bubbles and turbulence, then fell—slightly tail-first—for a short distance before large bags popped out under each delta wing. Then it bobbed up to about our level and stayed.

"This is Captain Stott. Now listen carefully. There is a beach some twenty-eight klicks from your present position, in the direction of the enemy. You will be proceeding to this beach by scoutship and from there will mount your assault on the Tauran position." That was *some* improvement; we'd only have to walk eighty klicks.

We deflated the bags, blasted to the surface and flew in a slow, spread-out formation to the beach. It took several minutes. As the ship scraped to a halt, I could hear pumps humming, making the cabin pressure equal to the air pressure outside. Before it had quite stopped moving, the escape slot beside my couch slid open. I rolled out onto the wing of the craft and jumped to the ground. Ten seconds to find cover—I sprinted across loose gravel to the "treeline," a twisty bramble of tall sparse bluish-green shrubs. I dove into the briar patch and turned to watch the ships leave. The drones that were left rose slowly to about a hundred meters, then took off in all directions with a bone-jarring roar. The real scout-ships slid slowly back into the water. Maybe that was a good idea.

It wasn't a terribly attractive world but certainly would be eas-ier to get around in than the cryogenic nightmare we were trained for. The sky was a uniform dull silver brightness that merged with the mist over the ocean so completely it was impossible to tell where water ended and air began. Small wavelets licked at the black gravel shore, much too slow and graceful in the three-quarters Earth-normal gravity. Even from fifty meters away, the rattle of billions of pebbles rolling with the tide was loud in my ears.

The air temperature was 79 degrees Centigrade, not quite hot enough for the sea to boil, even though the air pressure was low compared to Earth's. Wisps of steam drifted quickly upward from the line where water met land. I wondered how a lone man would survive exposed here without a suit. Would the heat or the low oxygen (partial pressure one-eighth Earth normal) kill him first? Or was there some deadly microorganism that would beat them both . . . ?

"This is Cortez. Everybody come over and assemble on me." He was standing on the beach a little to the left of me, waving his hand in a circle over his head. I walked toward him through the shrubs. They were brittle, unsubstantial, seemed paradoxically dried-out in the steamy air. They wouldn't offer much in the way of cover.

"We'll be advancing on a heading .05 radians east of north. I want Platoon One to take point. Two and Three follow about twenty meters behind, to the left and right. Seven, command pla-toon, is in the middle, twenty meters behind Two and Three. Five and Six, bring up the rear, in a semicircular closed flank. Every-body straight?" Sure, we could do that "arrowhead" maneuver in our sleep. "OK, let's move out."

I was in Platoon Seven, the "command group." Captain Stott put me there not because I was expected to give any commands, but because of my training in physics.

The command group was supposedly the safest place, buffered by six platoons: people were assigned to it because there was some tactical reason for them to survive at least a little longer than the rest. Cortez was there to give orders. Chavez was there to correct suit malfunctions. The senior medic, Doc Wilson (the only medic who actually had an M.D.), was there, and so was Theodopolis, the radio engineer, our link with the captain, who had elected to stay in orbit.

The rest of us were assigned to the command group by dint of special training or aptitude that wouldn't normally be considered of a "tactical" nature. Facing a totally unknown enemy, there was no way of telling what might prove important. Thus I was there because I was the closest the company had to a physicist. Rogers was biology. Tate was chemistry. Ho could crank out a perfect score on the Rhine extrasensory perception test, every time. Bohrs was a polyglot, able to speak twenty-one languages fluently, idiomatically. Petrov's talent was that he had tested out to have not one molecule of xenophobia in his psyche. Keating was a skilled acrobat. Debby Hollister—"Lucky" Hollister—showed a remarkable aptitude for making money, and also had a consistently high Rhine potential.

When we first set out, we were using the "jungle" camouflage combination on our suits. But what passed for jungle in these anemic tropics was too sparse; we looked like a band of conspicuous harlequins trooping through the woods. Cortez had us switch to black, but that was just as bad, as the light of Epsilon came evenly from all parts of the sky, and there were no shadows except ours. We finally settled on the dun-colored desert camouflage.

The nature of the countryside changed slowly as we walked north, away from the sea. The thorned stalks—I guess you could call them trees—came in fewer numbers but were bigger around and less brittle; at the base of each was a tangled mass of vine with the same bluegreen color, which spread out in a flattened cone some ten meters in diameter. There was a delicate green flower the size of a man's head near the top of each tree.

Grass began to grow some five klicks from the sea. It seemed to respect the trees' "property rights," leaving a strip of bare earth around each cone of vine. At the edge of such a clearing, it would grow as timid bluegreen stubble, then, moving away from the tree, would get thicker and taller until it reached shoulderhigh in some places, where the separation between two trees was unusually large. The grass was a lighter, greener shade than the trees and vines. We changed the color of our suits to the bright green we had used for maximum visibility on Charon. Keeping to the thickest part of the grass, we were fairly inconspicuous.

We covered over twenty klicks each day, buoyant after months under two gees. Until the second day, the only form of animal life we saw was a kind of black worm, finger-sized, with hundreds of cilium legs like the bristles of a brush. Rogers said that there obviously had to be some larger creature around, or there would be no reason for the trees to have thorns. So we were doubly on guard, expecting trouble both from the Taurans and the unidentified "large creature."

Potter's second platoon was on point; the general freak was reserved for her, since her platoon would likely be the first to spot any trouble.

"Sarge, this is Potter," we all heard. "Movement ahead."

"Get down, then!"

"We are. Don't think they see us."

"First platoon, go up to the right of point. Keep down. Fourth, get up to the left. Tell me when you get in position. Sixth platoon, stay back and guard the rear. Fifth and third, close with the command group."

Two dozen people whispered out of the grass to join us. Cortez must have heard from the fourth platoon.

"Good. How about you, first? . . . OK, fine. How many are there?"

"Eight we can see." Potter's voice.

"Good. When I give the word, open fire. Shoot to kill."

"Sarge, . . . they're just animals."

"Potter—if you've known all this time what a Tauran looks like, you should've told us. Shoot to kill."

"But we need . . ."

"We need a prisoner, but we don't need to escort him forty klicks to his home base and keep an eye on him while we fight. Clear?"

"Yes. Sergeant."

"OK. Seventh, all you brains and weirds, we're going up and watch. Fifth and third, come along to guard."

We crawled through the meter-high grass to where the second platoon had stretched out in a firing line.

"I don't see anything," Cortez said.

"Ahead and just to the left. Dark green."

They were only a shade darker than the grass. But after you saw the first one, you could see them all, moving slowly around some thirty meters ahead.

"Fire!" Cortez fired first; then twelve streaks of crimson leaped out and the grass wilted black, disappeared, and the creatures convulsed and died trying to scatter.

"Hold fire, hold it!" Cortez stood up. "We want to have something left—second platoon, follow me." He strode out toward the smoldering corpses, laser-finger pointed out front, obscene divining rod pulling him toward the carnage. . . . I felt my gorge rising and knew that all the lurid training tapes, all the horrible deaths in training accidents, hadn't prepared me for this sudden reality . . . that I had a magic wand that I could point at a life and make it a smoking piece of half-raw meat; I wasn't a soldier nor ever wanted to be one nor ever would want—

"OK, seventh, come on up." While we were walking toward them, one of the creatures moved, a tiny shudder, and Cortez flicked the beam of his laser over it with an almost negligent gesture. It made a hand-deep gash across the creature's middle. It died, like the others, without emitting a sound.

They were not quite as tall as humans, but wider in girth. They were covered with dark green, almost black, fur—white curls where the laser had singed. They appeared to have three legs and an arm. The only ornament to their shaggy heads was a mouth, wet black orifice filled with flat black teeth. They were thoroughly repulsive, but their worst feature was not a difference from human beings, but a similarity. . . . Whenever the laser had opened a body cavity, milk-white glistening veined globes and coils of organs spilled out, and their blood was dark clotting red.

"Rogers, take a look. Taurans or not?"

Rogers knelt by one of the disemboweled creatures and opened a flat plastic box, filled with glittering dissecting tools. She selected a scalpel. "One way we might be able to find out." Doc Wilson watched over her shoulder as she methodically slit the membrane covering several organs.

"Here." She held up a blackish fibrous mass between two fingers, a parody of daintiness through all that armor.

"So?"

"It's grass, Sergeant. If the Taurans eat the grass and breathe the air, they certainly found a planet remarkably like their home." She tossed it away. "They're animals, Sergeant, just fucken animals."

"I don't know," Doc Wilson said. "Just because they walk around on all fours, threes maybe, and eat grass . . ."

"Well, let's check out the brain." She found one that had been hit in the head and scraped the superficial black char from the wound. "Look at that."

It was almost solid bone. She tugged and ruffled the hair all over the head of another one. "What the hell does it use for sensory organs? No eyes, or ears, or . . ." She stood up.

"Nothing in that fucken head but a mouth and ten centimeters of skull. To protect nothing, not a fucken thing."

"If I could shrug, I'd shrug," the doctor said. "It doesn't prove anything—a brain doesn't have to look like a mushy walnut and it doesn't have to be in the head. Maybe that skull isn't bone, maybe *that's* the brain, some crystal lattice . . ."

"Yeah, but the fucken stomach's in the right place, and if those aren't intestines I'll eat—"

"Look," Cortez said, "this is real interesting, but all we need to know is whether that thing's dangerous, then we've gotta move on; we don't have all—"

"They aren't dangerous," Rogers began. "They don't—"

"Medic! DOC!" Somebody back at the firing line was waving his arms. Doc sprinted back to him, the rest of us following.

"What's wrong?" He had reached back and unclipped his medical kit on the run.

"It's Ho. She's out."

Doc swung open the door on Ho's biomedical monitor. He didn't have to look far. "She's dead."

"Dead?" Cortez said. "What the hell—"

"Just a minute." Doc plugged a jack into the monitor and fiddled with some dials on his kit. "Everybody's biomed readout is stored for twelve hours. I'm running it backwards, should be able to—there!"

"What?"

"Four and a half minutes ago—must have been when you opened fire—Jesus!"

"Well?"

"Massive cerebral hemorrhage. No . . ." He watched the dials. "No . . . warning, no indication of anything out of the ordinary; blood pressure up, pulse up, but normal under the circumstances . . . nothing to . . . indicate—" He reached down and popped her suit. Her fine oriental features were distorted in a horrible grimace, both gums showing. Sticky fluid ran from under her collapsed eyelids, and a trickle of blood still dripped from each ear. Doc Wilson closed the suit back up.

"I've never seen anything like it. It's as if a bomb went off in her skull."

"Oh fuck," Rogers said, "she was Rhine-sensitive, wasn't she."

"That's right," Cortez sounded thoughtful. "All right, everybody listen up. Platoon leaders, check your platoons and see if anybody's missing, or hurt. Anybody else in seventh?"

"I . . . I've got a splitting headache, Sarge," Lucky said.

Four others had bad headaches. One of them affirmed that he was slightly Rhine-sensitive. The others didn't know.

"Cortez, I think it's obvious," Doc Wilson said, "that we should give these . . . monsters wide berth, especially shouldn't harm any more of them. Not with five people susceptible to whatever apparently killed Ho."

"Of course, God damn it, I don't need anybody to tell me that. We'd better get moving. I just filled the captain in on what happened; he agrees that we'd better get as far away from here as we can, before we stop for the night.

"Let's get back in formation and continue on the same bearing. Fifth platoon, take over point; second, come back to the rear. Everybody else, same as before."

"What about Ho?" Lucky asked.

"She'll be taken care of. From the ship."

After we'd gone half a klick, there was a flash and rolling thunder. Where Ho had been came a wispy luminous mushroom cloud boiling up to disappear against the gray sky.

We stopped for the "night"—actually, the sun wouldn't set for another seventy hours—atop a slight rise some ten klicks from where we had killed the aliens. But they weren't aliens, I had to remind myself—*we* were.

Two platoons deployed in a ring around the rest of us, and we flopped down exhausted. Everybody was allowed four hours' sleep and had two hours' guard duty.

Potter came over and sat next to me. I chinned her frequency.

"Hi, Marygay."

"Oh, William," her voice over the radio was hoarse and cracking. "God, it's so horrible."

"It's over now—"

"I killed one of them, the first instant, I shot it right in the, in the . . ."

I put my hand on her knee. The contact had a plastic click and I jerked it back, visions of machines embracing, copulating. "Don't feel singled out, Marygay; whatever guilt there is, is . . . belongs evenly to all of us, . . . but a triple portion for Cor—"

"You privates quit jawin' and get some sleep. You both pull guard in two hours."

"OK, Sarge." Her voice was so sad and tired I couldn't bear it. I felt if I could only touch her, I could drain off the sadness like ground wire draining current, but we were each trapped in our own plastic world—

"G'night, William."

"Night." It's almost impossible to get sexually excited inside a suit, with the relief tube and all the silver chloride sensors poking you, but somehow this was my body's response to the emotional impotence, maybe remembering more pleasant sleeps with Mary-gay, maybe feeling that in the midst of all this death, personal death could be very soon, cranking up the procreative derrick for one last try . . . lovely thoughts like this. I fell asleep and dreamed that I was a machine, mimicking the functions of life, creaking and clanking my clumsy way through a world, people too polite to say anything but giggling behind my back, and the little man who sat inside my head pulling the levers and clutches and watching the dials, he was hopelessly mad and was storing up hurts for the day—

"Mandella—wake up, goddammit, your shift!"

I shuffled over to my place on the perimeter to watch for god knows what . . . but I was so weary I couldn't keep my eyes open. Finally I tongued a stimtab, knowing I'd pay for it later.

For over an hour I sat there, scanning my sector left, right, near, far, the scene never changing, not even a breath of wind to stir the grass.

Then suddenly the grass parted and one of the three-legged creatures was right in front of me. I raised my finger but didn't squeeze.

"Movement!"

"Movement!"

"Jesus Chri—there's one right—"

"HOLD YOUR FIRE! F' shit's sake don't shoot!"

"Movement."

"Movement." I looked left and right, and as far as I could see, every perimeter guard had one of the blind, dumb creatures standing right in front of him.

Maybe the drug I'd taken to stay awake made me more sensitive to whatever they did. My scalp crawled and I felt a formless *thing* in my mind, the feeling you get when somebody has said something and you didn't quite hear it, want to respond, but the opportunity to ask him to repeat it is gone.

The creature sat back on its haunches, leaning forward on the one front leg. Big green bear with a withered arm. Its power threaded through my mind, spiderwebs, echo of night terrors, trying to communicate, trying to destroy me, I couldn't know.

"All right, everybody on the perimeter, fall back, slow. Don't make any quick gestures. . . . Anybody got a headache or anything?"

"Sergeant, this is Hollister." Lucky.

"They're trying to say something . . . I can almost . . . no, just . . ."

"All I can get is that they think we're, think we're . . . well, *funny*. They're not afraid."

"You mean the one in front of you isn't—"

"No, the feeling comes from all of them, they're all thinking the same thing. Don't ask me how I know, I just do."

"Maybe they thought it was funny, what they did to Ho."

"Maybe. I don't feel they're dangerous. Just curious about us."

"Sergeant, this is Bohrs."

"Yeah."

"The Taurans've been here at least a year—maybe they've learned how to communicate with these . . . overgrown teddy bears. They might be spying on us, might be sending back—"

"I don't think they'd show themselves if that were the case," Lucky said. "They can obviously hide from us pretty well when they want to."

"Anyhow," Cortez said, "if they're spies, the damage has been done. Don't think it'd be smart to take any action against them. I know you'd all like to see 'em dead for what they did to Ho, so would I, but we'd better be careful."

I didn't want to see them dead, but I'd just as soon not have seen them in any condition. I was walking backwards slowly, toward the middle of camp. The creature didn't seem disposed to follow. Maybe he just knew we were surrounded. He was pulling up grass with his arm and munching.

"OK, all of you platoon leaders, wake everybody up, get a roll count. Let me know if anybody's been hurt. Tell your people we're moving out in one minute."

I don't know what Cortez had expected, but of course the creatures followed right along. They didn't keep us surrounded; just had twenty or thirty following us all the time. Not the same ones, either. Individuals would saunter away, and new ones would join the parade. It was pretty obvious that *they* weren't going to tire out.

We were each allowed one stimtab. Without it, no one could have marched an hour. A second pill would have been welcome after the edge started to wear off, but the mathematics of the situation forbade it; we were still thirty klicks from the enemy base, fifteen hours' marching at the least. And though you could stay awake and energetic for a hundred hours on the tabs, aberrations of judgment and perception snowballed after the second one, until *in extremis* the most bizarre hallucinations would be taken at face value, and a person could fidget for hours deciding whether to have breakfast.

Under artificial stimulation, the company traveled with great energy for the first six hours, was slowing by the seventh, and ground to an exhausted halt after nine hours and nineteen kilometers. The teddy bears had never lost sight of us and, according to Lucky, had never stopped "broadcasting." Cortez's decision was that we would stop for seven hours, each platoon taking one hour of perimeter guard. I was never so glad to have been in the seventh platoon, as we stood guard the last shift and thus were able to get six hours of uninterrupted sleep.

In the few moments I lay awake after finally lying down, the thought came to me that the next time I closed my eyes could well be the last. And partly because of the drug hangover, mostly because of the past day's horrors, I found that I really didn't give a shit.

Our first contact with the Taurans came during my shift.

The teddy bears were still there when I woke up and replaced Doc Jones on guard. They'd gone back to their original formation, one in front of each guard position. The one who was waiting for me seemed a little larger than normal, but otherwise looked just like all the others. All the grass had been cropped where he was sitting, so he occasionally made forays to the left or right. But he always returned to sit right in front of me, you would say *staring* if he had had anything to stare with.

We had been facing each other for about fifteen minutes when Cortez's voice rumbled:

"Awright everybody, wake up and get hid!"

I followed instinct and flopped to the ground and rolled into a tall stand of grass.

"Enemy vessel overhead." His voice was almost laconic.

Strictly speaking, it wasn't really overhead, but rather passing somewhat east of us. It was moving slowly, maybe a hundred klicks per hour, and looked like a broomstick surrounded by a dirty soap bubble. The creature riding it was a little more human-looking than the teddy bears, but still no prize. I cranked my image amplifier up to forty log two for a closer look.

He had two arms and two legs, but his waist was so small you could encompass it with both hands. Under the tiny waist was a large horse-shoe-shaped pelvic structure nearly a meter wide, from which dangled two long skinny legs with no apparent knee joint. Above that waist his body swelled out again, to a chest no smaller than the huge pelvis. His arms looked surprisingly human, except that they were too long and undermuscled. There were too many fingers on his hands. Shoulderless, neckless. His head was a nightmarish growth that swelled like a goiter from his massive chest. Two eyes that looked like clusters of fish eggs, a bundle of tassles instead of a nose, and a rigidly open hole that might have been a mouth sitting low down where his adam's apple should have been. Evidently the soap bubble contained an amenable environment, as he was wearing absolutely nothing except his ridged hide, that looked like skin submerged too long in hot water, then dyed a pale orange. "He" had no external genitalia, but nothing that might hint of mammary glands. So we opted for the male pronoun by default.

Obviously, he either didn't see us or thought we were part of the herd of teddy bears. He never looked back at us, but just continued in the same direction we were headed, .05 rad east of north.

"Might as well go back to sleep now, if you can sleep after looking at *that* thing. We move out at 0435." Forty minutes.

Because of the planet's opaque cloud cover, there had been no way to tell, from space, what the enemy base looked like or how big it was. We only knew its position, the same way we knew the position the scoutships were supposed to land on. So it too could easily have been underwater, or underground.

But some of the drones were reconnaissance ships as well as decoys: and in their mock attacks on the base, one managed to get close enough to take a picture. Captain Stott beamed down a diagram of the place to Cortez—the only one with a visor in his suit—when we were five klicks from the base's "radio" position. We stopped and he called all the platoon leaders in with the seventh platoon to confer. Two teddy bears loped in, too. We tried to ignore them.

"OK, the captain sent down some pictures of our objective. I'm going to draw a map; you platoon leaders copy." They took pads and styli out of their leg pockets, while Cortez unrolled a large plastic mat. He gave it a shake to randomize any residual charge, and turned on his stylus.

"Now, we're coming from this direction." He put an arrow at the bottom of the sheet. "First thing we'll hit is this row of huts, probably billets or bunkers, but who the hell knows. . . . Our initial objective is to destroy these buildings—the whole base is on a flat plain; there's no way we could really sneak by them."

"Potter here. Why can't we jump over them?"

"Yeah, we could do that, and wind up completely surrounded, cut to ribbons. We take the buildings.

"After we do that . . . all I can say is that we'll have to think on our feet. From the aerial reconnaissance, we can figure out the function of only a couple of buildings—and that stinks. We might wind up wasting a lot of time demolishing the equivalent of an enlisted-men's bar, ignoring a huge logistic computer because it looks like . . . a garbage dump or something."

"Mandella here," I said. "Isn't there a spaceport of some kind—seems to me we ought to . . ."

"I'll *get* to that, damn it. There's a ring of these huts all around the camp, so we've got to break through somewhere. This place'll be closest, less chance of giving away our position before we attack.

"There's nothing in the whole place that actually looks like a weapon. That doesn't mean anything, though; you could hide a gigawatt laser in each of those huts.

"Now, about five hundred meters from the huts, in the middle of the base, we'll come to this big flower-shaped structure." Cortez drew a large symmetrical shape that looked like the outline of a flower with seven petals. "What the hell this is, your guess is as good as mine. There's only one of them, though, so we don't damage it any more than we have to. Which means . . . we blast it to splinters if I think it's dangerous.

"Now, as far as your spaceport, Mandella, is concerned—there just isn't one. Nothing.

"That cruiser the *Hope* caulked had probably been left in orbit, like ours has to be. If they have any equivalent of a scoutship, or drone missiles, they're either not kept here or they're well hidden."

"Bohrs here. Then what did they attack with, while we were coming down from orbit?"

"I wish we knew, Private.

"Obviously, we don't have any way of estimating their numbers, not directly. Recon pictures failed to show a single Tauran on the grounds of the base. Meaning nothing, because it *is* an alien environment. Indirectly, though . . . we count the number of broomsticks, those flying things.

"There are fifty-one huts, and each has at most one broomstick. Four don't have any parked outside, but we located three at various other parts of the base. Maybe this indicates that there are fifty-one Taurans, one of whom was outside the base when the picture was taken."

"Keating here. Or fifty-one officers."

"That's right—maybe fifty thousand infantrymen stacked in one of these buildings. No way to tell. Maybe ten Taurans, each with five broomsticks, to use according to his mood.

"We've got one thing in our favor, and that's communications. They evidently use a frequency modulation of megahertz electromagnetic radiation."

"Radio!"

"That's right, whoever you are. Identify yourself when you speak. So it's quite possible that they can't detect our phased-neutrino communications. Also, just prior to the attack, the *Hope* is going to deliver a nice dirty fission bomb; detonate it in the upper atmosphere right over the base. That'll restrict them to line-of-sight communications for some time; even those will be full of static."

"Why don't . . . Tate here . . . why don't they just drop the bomb right in their laps. Save us a lot of—"

"That doesn't even deserve an answer, Private. But the answer is, they might. And you better hope they don't. If they caulk the base, it'll be for the safety of the *Hope. After* we've attacked, and probably before we're far enough away for it to make much difference.

"We keep that from happening by doing a good job. We have to reduce the base to where it can no longer function; at the same time, leave as much intact as possible. And take one prisoner."

"Potter here. You mean, at least one prisoner."

"I mean what I say. One only. Potter . . . you're relieved of your platoon. Send Chavez up."

"All right, Sergeant." The relief in her voice was unmistakable.

Cortez continued with his map and instructions. There was one other building whose function was pretty obvious; it had a large steerable dish antenna on top. We were to destroy it as soon as the grenadiers got in range.

The attack plan was very loose. Our signal to begin would be the flash of the fission bomb. At the same time, several drones would converge on the base, so we could see what their antispacecraft defenses were. We would try to reduce the effectiveness of those defenses without destroying them completely.

Immediately after the bomb and the drones, the grenadiers would vaporize a line of seven huts. Everybody would break through the hole into the base . . . and what would happen after that was anybody's guess.

Ideally, we'd sweep from that end of the base to the other, destroying certain targets, caulking all but one Tauran. But that was unlikely to happen, as it depended on the Taurans' offering very little resistance.

On the other hand, if the Taurans showed obvious superiority from the beginning, Cortez would give the order to scatter. Everybody had a different compass bearing for retreat—we'd blossom out in all directions, the survivors to rendezvous in a valley some forty klicks east of the base. Then we'd see about a return engagement, after the *Hope* softened the base up a bit.

"One last thing," Cortez rasped. "Maybe some of you feel the way Potter evidently does, maybe some of your men feel that way . . . that we ought to go easy, not make this so much of a bloodbath. Mercy is a luxury, a weakness we can't afford to indulge in at this stage of the war. *All* we know about the enemy is that they have killed seven hundred and ninety-eight humans. They haven't shown any restraint in attacking our cruisers, and it'd be foolish to expect any this time, this first ground action.

"*They* are responsible for the lives of all of your comrades who died in training, and for Ho, and for all the others who are surely going to die today. I can't *understand* anybody who wants to spare them. But that doesn't make any difference. You have your orders and, what the hell, you might as well know, all of you have a post-hypnotic suggestion that I will trigger by a phrase, just before the battle. It will make your job easier."

"Sergeant . . ."

"Shut up. We're short on time; get back to your platoons and brief them. We move out in five minutes."

The platoon leaders returned to their men, leaving Cortez and ten of us—plus three teddy bears, milling around, getting in the way.

We took the last five klicks very carefully, sticking to the highest grass, running across occasional clearings. When we were 500 meters from where the base was supposed to be, Cortez took the third platoon forward to scout, while the rest of us laid low.

Cortez's voice came over the general freak: "Looks pretty much like we expected. Advance in a file, crawling. When you get to the third platoon, follow your squad leader to the left or right."

We did that and wound up with a string of eighty-three people in a line roughly perpendicular to the direction of attack. We were pretty well hidden, except for the dozen or so teddy bears that mooched along the line, munching grass.

There was no sign of life inside the base. All of the buildings were windowless and a uniform shiny white. The huts that were our first objective were large featureless half-buried eggs some sixty meters apart. Cortez assigned one to each grenadier.

We were broken into three fire teams: team A consisted of platoons two, four, and six; team B was one, three, and five; the command platoon was team C.

"Less than a minute now—filters down!—when I say 'fire,' grenadiers, take out your targets. God help you if you miss."

There was a sound like a giant's belch, and a stream of five or six iridescent bubbles floated up from the flower-shaped building. They rose with increasing speed until they were almost out of sight, then shot off to the south, over our heads. The ground was suddenly bright, and for the first time in a long time, I saw my shadow, a long one pointed north. The bomb had gone off prema-

turely. I just had time to think that it didn't make too much difference; it'd still make alphabet soup out of their communications—

"Drones!" A ship came screaming in just about tree level, and
a bubble was in the air to meet it. When they contacted, the bubble
popped and the drone exploded into a million tiny fragments. Another one came from the opposite side and suffered the same fate.

"FIRE!" Seven bright glares of 500-microton grenades and a
sustained concussion that surely would have killed an unpro-
tected man.

"Filters up." Gray haze of smoke and dust. Clods of dirt
falling with a sound like heavy raindrops.

"Listen up:

> *'Scots, wha hae wi' Wallace bled;*
> *Scots, wham Bruce has aften led,*
> *Welcome to your gory bed,*
> *Or to victory!'* "

I hardly heard him for trying to keep track of what was going
on in my skull. I knew it was just post-hypnotic suggestion, even
remembered the session in Missouri when they'd implanted it, but
that didn't make it any less compelling. My mind reeled under the
strong pseudo-memories: shaggy hulks that were Taurans (not at
all what we now knew they looked like) boarding a colonists' vessel, eating babies while mothers watched in screaming terror (the
colonists never took babies; they wouldn't stand the acceleration),
then raping the women to death with huge veined purple members
(ridiculous that they would feel desire for humans), holding the
men down while they plucked flesh from their living bodies and
gobbled it (as if they could assimilate the alien protein) . . . a hundred grisly details as sharply remembered as the events of a
minute ago, ridiculously overdone and logically absurd. But while
my conscious mind was rejecting the silliness, somewhere much
deeper, down in that sleeping animal where we keep our real mo-
tives and morals, something was thirsting for alien blood, secure
in the conviction that the noblest thing a man could do would be to
die killing one of those horrible monsters. . . .

I knew it was all purest soyashit, and I hated the men who had
taken such obscene liberties with my mind, but I could even *hear*
my teeth grinding, feel my cheeks frozen in a spastic grin, blood-
lust . . . A teddy bear walked in front of me, looking dazed. I

started to raise my laser-finger, but somebody beat me to it and the creature's head exploded in a cloud of gray splinters and blood.

Lucky groaned, half-whining, "Dirty . . . filthy fucken bastards." Lasers flared and crisscrossed, and all of the teddy bears fell dead.

"*Watch* it, goddammit," Cortez screamed. "*Aim* those fuckin things—they aren't toys!

"Team *A*, move out—into the craters to cover *B*."

Somebody was laughing and sobbing. "What the fuck is wrong with *you*, Petrov?" Strange to hear Cortez cussing.

I twisted around and saw Petrov, behind and to my left, lying in a shallow hole, digging frantically with both hands, crying and gurgling.

"Fuck," Cortez said. "Team *B*! Ten meters past the craters, get down in a line. Team *C*—into the craters with *A*."

I scrambled up and covered the hundred meters in twelve amplified strides. The craters were practically large enough to hide a scoutship, some ten meters in diameter. I jumped to the opposite side of the hole and landed next to a fellow named Chin. He didn't even look around when I landed, just kept scanning the base for signs of life.

"Team *A*—ten meters, past team *B*, down in line." Just as he finished, the building in front of us burped, and a salvo of the bubbles fanned out toward our lines. Most people saw it coming and got down, but Chin was just getting up to make his rush and stepped right into one.

It grazed the top of his helmet and disappeared with a faint pop. He took one step backwards and toppled over the edge of the crater, trailing an arc of blood and brains. Lifeless, spread-eagled, he slid halfway to the bottom, shoveling dirt into the perfectly symmetrical hole where the bubble had chewed indiscriminately through plastic, hair, skin, bone, and brain.

"Everybody hold it. Platoon leaders, casualty report . . . check . . . check, check . . . check, check, check . . . check. We have three deaders. Wouldn't be *any* if you'd have kept low. So everybody grab dirt when you hear that thing go off. Team *A*, complete the rush."

They completed the maneuver without incident. "OK. Team *C*, rush to where *B* . . . hold it! Down!"

Everybody was already hugging the ground. The bubbles slid by in a smooth arc about two meters off the ground. They went serenely over our heads and, except for one that made toothpicks out of a tree, disappeared in the distance.

"*B*, rush past *A* ten meters. *C*, take over *B*'s place. You *B* grenadiers, see if you can reach the Flower."

Two grenades tore up the ground thirty or forty meters from the structure. In a good imitation of panic, it started belching out a continuous stream of bubbles—still, none coming lower than two meters off the ground. We kept hunched down and continued to advance.

Suddenly, a seam appeared in the building and widened to the size of a large door. Taurans came swarming out.

"Grenadiers, hold your fire. *B* team, laser fire to the left and right—keep'm bunched up. *A* and *C*, rush down the center."

One Tauran died trying to run through a laser beam. The others stayed where they were.

In a suit, it's pretty awkward to run and keep your head down at the same time. You have to go from side to side, like a skater getting started; otherwise you'll be airborne. At least one person, somebody in *A* team, bounced too high and suffered the same fate as Chin.

I was feeling pretty fenced-in and trapped, with a wall of laser fire on each side and a low ceiling that meant death to touch. But in spite of myself, I felt happy, euphoric, finally getting the chance to kill some of those villainous baby-eaters. Knowing it was soyashit.

They weren't fighting back, except for the rather ineffective bubbles (obviously not designed as an anti-personnel weapon), and they didn't retreat back into the building, either. They milled around, about a hundred of them, and watched us get closer. A couple of grenades would caulk them all, but I guess Cortez was thinking about the prisoner.

"OK, when I say 'go,' we're going to flank 'em. *B* team will hold fire . . . Second and fourth platoons to the right, sixth and seventh to the left. *B* team will move forward in line to box them in.

"Go!" We peeled off to the left. As soon as the lasers stopped, the Taurans bolted, running in a group on a collision course with our flank.

"*A* team, down and fire! Don't shoot until you're sure of your aim—if you miss you might hit a friendly. And fer Chris' sake save me one!"

It was a horrifying sight, that herd of monsters bearing down on us. They were running in great leaps—the bubbles avoiding them—and they all looked like the one we saw earlier, riding the broomstick; naked except for an almost transparent sphere around their whole bodies, that moved along with them. The right flank started firing, picking off individuals in the rear of the pack.

Suddenly a laser flared through the Taurans from the other side, somebody missing his mark. There was a horrible scream, and I looked down the line to see someone—I think it was Perry—writhing on the ground, right hand over the smoldering stump of his arm, seared off just below the elbow. Blood sprayed through his fingers, and the suit, its camouflage circuits scrambled, flickered black-white-jungle-desert-green-gray. I don't know how long I stared—long enough for the medic to run over and start giving aid—but when I looked up the Taurans were almost on top of me.

My first shot was wild and high, but it grazed the top of the leading Tauran's protective bubble. The bubble disappeared and the monster stumbled and fell to the ground, jerking spasmodically. Foam gushed out of his mouth-hole, first white, then streaked red. With one last jerk he became rigid and twisted backwards, almost to the shape of a horseshoe. His long scream, a high-pitched whistle, stopped just as his comrades trampled over him. I hated myself for smiling.

It was slaughter, even though our flank was outnumbered five to one. They kept coming without faltering, even when they had to climb over the drift of bodies and parts of bodies that piled up high, parallel to our flank. The ground between us was slick red with Tauran blood—all God's children got hemoglobin—and like the teddy bears, their guts looked pretty much like guts to my untrained eye. My helmet reverberated with hysterical laughter while we slashed them to gory chunks, and I almost didn't hear Cortez:

"Hold your fire—I said HOLD IT, goddammit! *Catch* a couple of the bastards, they won't hurt you."

I stopped shooting and eventually so did everybody else. When the next Tauran jumped over the smoking pile of meat in front of me, I dove to try to tackle him around those spindly legs.

It was like hugging a big, slippery balloon. When I tried to drag him down, he popped out of my arms and kept running.

We managed to stop one of them by the simple expedient of piling half-a-dozen people on top of him. By that time the others had run through our line and were headed for the row of large cylindrical tanks that Cortez had said were probably for storage. A little door had opened in the base of each one.

"We've *got* our prisoner," Cortez shouted. *"Kill!"*

They were fifty meters away and running hard, difficult targets. Lasers slashed around them, bobbing high and low. One fell, sliced in two, but the others, about ten of them, kept going and were almost to the doors when the grenadiers started firing.

They were still loaded with 500-mike bombs, but a near miss wasn't enough—the concussion would just send them flying, unhurt in their bubbles.

"The buildings! Get the fucken buildings!" The grenadiers raised their aim and let fly, but the bombs only seemed to scorch the white outside of the structures until, by chance, one landed in a door. That split the building just as if it had a seam; the two halves popped away and a cloud of machinery flew into the air, accompanied by a huge pale flame that rolled up and disappeared in an instant. Then the others all concentrated on the doors, except for potshots at some of the Taurans, not so much to get them as to blow them away before they could get inside. They seemed awfully eager.

All this time, we were trying to get the Taurans with laser fire, while they weaved and bounced around trying to get into the structures. We moved in as close to them as we could without putting ourselves in danger from the grenade blasts, yet too far away for good aim.

Still, we were getting them one by one and managed to destroy four of the seven buildings. Then, when there were only two aliens left, a nearby grenade blast flung one of them to within a few meters of a door. He dove in and several grenadiers fired salvos after him, but they all fell short or detonated harmlessly on the side. Bombs were falling all around, making an awful racket, but the sound was suddenly drowned out by a great sigh, like a giant's intake of breath, and where the building had been was a thick cylindrical cloud of smoke, solid-looking, dwindling away into the stratosphere, straight as if laid down by a ruler. The other Tauran had been right at the base of the cylinder; I could see pieces of him flying. A second later, a shock wave hit us and I rolled helplessly, pinwheeling, to smash into the pile of Tauran bodies and roll beyond.

I picked myself up and panicked for a second when I saw there was blood all over my suit—when I realized it was only alien blood, I relaxed but felt unclean.

"*Catch* the bastard! Catch him!" In the confusion, the Tauran had gotten free and was running for the grass. One platoon was chasing after him, losing ground, but then all of *B* team ran over and cut him off. I jogged over to join in the fun.

There were four people on top of him, and a ring around them of about fifty people, watching the struggle.

"Spread out, dammit! There might be a thousand more of them waiting to get us in one place." We dispersed, grumbling. By unspoken agreement we were all sure that there were no more live Taurans on the face of the planet.

Cortez was walking toward the prisoner while I backed away. Suddenly the four men collapsed in a pile on top of the creature . . . Even from my distance I could see the foam spouting from his mouth-hole. His bubble had popped. Suicide.

"Damn!" Cortez was right there. "Get off that bastard." The four men got off and Cortez used his laser to slice the monster into a dozen quivering chunks. Heart-warming sight.

"That's all right, though, we'll find another one—everybody! Back in the arrowhead formation. Combat assault, on the Flower."

Well, we assaulted the Flower, which had evidently run out of ammunition (it was still belching, but no bubbles), and it was empty. We scurried up ramps and through corridors, fingers at the ready, like kids playing soldier. There was nobody home.

The same lack of response at the antenna installation, the "Salami," and twenty other major buildings, as well as the forty-four perimeter huts still intact. So we had "captured" dozens of buildings, mostly of incomprehensible purpose, but failed in our main mission, capturing a Tauran for the xenologists to experiment with. Oh well, they could have all the bits and pieces they'd ever want. That was something.

After we'd combed every last square centimeter of the base, a scoutship came in with the real exploration crew, the scientists. Cortez said, "All right, snap out of it," and the hypnotic compulsion fell away.

At first it was pretty grim. A lot of the people, like Lucky and Marygay, almost went crazy with the memories of bloody murder multiplied a hundred times. Cortez ordered everybody to take a sed-tab, two for the ones most upset. I took two without being specifically ordered to do so.

Because it *was* murder, unadorned butchery—once we had the anti-spacecraft weapon doped out, we hadn't been in any danger. The Taurans hadn't seemed to have any conception of person-to-person fighting. We had just herded them up and slaughtered them, the first encounter between mankind and another intelligent species. Maybe it was the second encounter, counting the teddy bears. What might have happened if we had sat down and tried to communicate? But they got the same treatment.

I spent a long time after that telling myself over and over that it hadn't been *me* who so gleefully carved up those frightened, stampeding creatures. Back in the twentieth century, they had established to everybody's satisfaction that "I was just following orders" was an inadequate excuse for inhuman conduct . . . but what can you do when the orders come from deep down in that puppet master of the unconscious?

Worst of all was the feeling that perhaps my actions weren't all that inhuman. Ancestors only a few generations back would have done the same thing, even to their fellow men, without any hypnotic conditioning.

I was disgusted with the human race, disgusted with the army and horrified at the prospect of living with myself for another century or so. . . . Well, there was always brain-wipe.

A ship with a lone Tauran survivor had escaped and had gotten away clean, the bulk of the planet shielding it from *Earth's Hope* while it dropped into Aleph's collapsar field. Escaped home, I guessed, wherever that was, to report what twenty men with hand-weapons could do to a hundred fleeing on foot, unarmed.

I suspected that the next time humans met Taurans in ground combat, we would be more evenly matched. And I was right.

Sergeant Mandella
2007–2024 A.D.

I was scared enough.

Sub-major Stott was pacing back and forth behind the small podium in the assembly room/chop hall/gymnasium of the *Anniversary*. We had just made our final collapsar jump, from Tet-38 to Yod-4. We were decelerating at 1½ gravities and our velocity relative to that collapsar was a respectable .90c. We were being chased.

"I wish you people would relax for a while and just trust the ship's computer. The Tauran vessel at any rate will not be within strike range for another two weeks. Mandella!"

He was always very careful to call me "Sergeant" Mandella in front of the company. But everybody at this particular briefing was either a sergeant or a corporal: squad leaders. "Yes, sir."

"You're responsible for the psychological as well as the physical well-being of the men and women in your squad. Assuming that you are aware that there is a morale problem aboard this vessel, what have you done about it?"

"As far as my squad is concerned, sir?"

"Of course."

"We talk it out, sir."

"And have you arrived at any cogent conclusion?"

"Meaning no disrespect, sir, I think the major problem is obvious. My people have been cooped up in this ship for fourteen—"

"Ridiculous! Every one of us has been adequately conditioned against the pressures of living in close quarters *and* the enlisted people have the privilege of confraternity." That was a delicate way of putting it. "Officers must remain celibate, and yet *we* have no morale problem."

If he thought his officers were celibate, he should sit down and have a long talk with Lieutenant Harmony. Maybe he just meant line officers, though. That would be just him and Cortez. Probably 50 percent right. Cortez was awfully friendly with Corporal Kamehameha.

"Sir, perhaps it was the detoxification back at Stargate; maybe—"

"No. The therapists only worked to erase the hate conditioning—everybody knows how *I* feel about that—and they may be misguided but they are skilled.

"Corporal Potter." He always called her by her rank to remind her why she hadn't been promoted as high as the rest of us. Too soft. "Have you 'talked it out' with your people, too?"

"We've discussed it, sir."

The sub-major could "glare mildly" at people. He glared mildly at Marygay until she elaborated.

"I don't believe it's the fault of the conditioning. My people are impatient, just tired of doing the same thing day after day."

"They're anxious for combat, then?" No sarcasm in his voice.

"They want to get off the ship, sir."

"They *will* get off the ship," he said, allowing himself a microscopic smile. "And then they'll probably be just as impatient to get back on."

It went back and forth like that for a long while. Nobody wanted to come right out and say that their squad was scared: scared of the Tauran cruiser closing on us, scared of the landing on the portal planet. Submajor Stott had a bad record of dealing with people who admitted fear.

I fingered the fresh T/O they had given us. It looked like this:

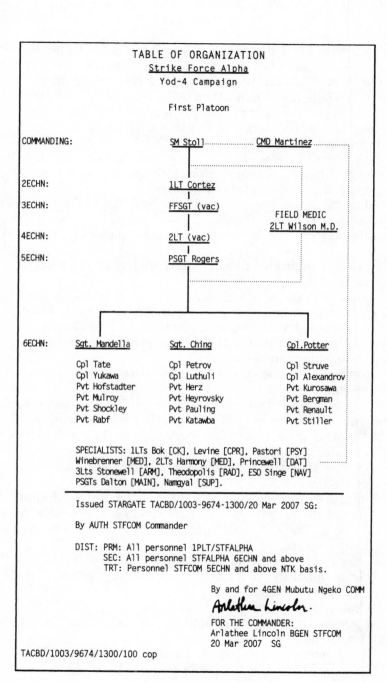

TABLE OF ORGANIZATION
Strike Force Alpha
Yod-4 Campaign

First Platoon

COMMANDING: SM Stoll................CMD Martinez............

2ECHN: 1LT Cortez

3ECHN: FFSGT (vac)
                                                FIELD MEDIC
                                                2LT Wilson M.D.
4ECHN: 2LT (vac)

5ECHN: PSGT Rogers

6ECHN: Sgt. Mandella   Sgt. Ching   Cpl.Potter

              Cpl Tate   Cpl Petrov   Cpl Struve
              Cpl Yukawa   Cpl Luthuli   Cpl Alexandrov
              Pvt Hofstadter   Pvt Herz   Pvt Kurosawa
              Pvt Mulroy   Pvt Heyrovsky   Pvt Bergman
              Pvt Shockley   Pvt Pauling   Pvt Renault
              Pvt Rabf   Pvt Katawba   Pvt Stiller

        SPECIALISTS: 1LTs Bok [CK], Levine [CPR], Pastori [PSY]
        Winebrenner [MED], 2LTs Harmony [MED], Princewell [DAT]
        3Lts Stonewell [ARM], Theodopolis [RAD], ESO Singe [NAV]
        PSGTs Dalton [MAIN], Namgyal [SUP].

        Issued STARGATE TACBD/1003-9674-1300/20 Mar 2007 SG:

        By AUTH STFCOM Commander

        DIST: PRM: All personnel 1PLT/STFALPHA
              SEC: All personnel STFALPHA 6ECHN and above
              TRT: Personnel STFCOM 5ECHN and above NTK basis.

                                By and for 4GEN Mubutu Ngeko COMM
                                Arlathee Lincoln.
                                FOR THE COMMANDER:
                                Arlathee Lincoln BGEN STFCOM
                                20 Mar 2007 SG

TACBD/1003/9674/1300/100 cop

I knew most of the people from the raid on Aleph, the first face-to-face contact between humans and Taurans. The only new people in my platoon were Luthuli and Heyrovsky. In the company as a whole (excuse me, the "strike force"), we had twenty replacements for the nineteen people we lost from the Aleph raid: one amputation, four deaders, fourteen psychotics.

I couldn't get over the "20 Mar 2007" at the bottom of the T/O. I'd been in the army ten years, though it felt like less than two. Time dilation, of course; even with the collapsar jumps, traveling from star to star eats up the calendar.

After this raid, I would probably be eligible for retirement, with full pay. If I lived through the raid, and if they didn't change the rules on us. Me a twenty-year man, and only twenty-five years old.

Stott was summing up when there was a knock on the door, a single loud rap. "Enter," he said.

An ensign I knew vaguely walked in casually and handed Stott a slip of paper, without saying a word. He stood there while Stott read it, slumping with just the right degree of insolence. Technically, Stott was out of his chain of command; everybody in the navy disliked him anyhow.

Stott handed the paper back to the ensign and looked through him.

"You will alert your squads that preliminary evasive maneuvers will commence at 2010, fifty-eight minutes from now." He hadn't looked at his watch. "All personnel will be in acceleration shells by 2000. Tench . . . hut!"

We rose and, without enthusiasm, chorused, "Fuck you, sir." Idiotic custom.

Stott strode out of the room and the ensign followed, smirking.

I turned my ring to my assistant squad leader's position and talked into it: "Tate, this is Mandella." Everyone else in the room was doing the same.

A tinny voice came out of the ring. "Tate here. What's up?"

"Get ahold of the men and tell them we have to be in the shells by 2000. Evasive maneuvers."

"Crap. They told us it would be days."

"I guess something new came up. Or maybe the Commodore has a bright idea."

"The Commodore can stuff it. You up in the lounge?"

"Yeah."

"Bring me back a cup when you come, okay? Little sugar?"

"Roger. Be down in about half an hour."

"Thanks. I'll get on it."

There was a general movement toward the coffee machine. I got in line behind Corporal Potter.

"What do you think, Marygay?"

"Maybe the Commodore just wants us to try out the shells once more."

"Before the real thing."

"Maybe." She picked up a cup and blew into it. She looked worried. "Or maybe the Taurans had a ship way out, waiting for us. I've wondered why they don't do it. We do, at Stargate."

"Stargate's a different thing. It takes seven cruisers, moving all the time, to cover all the possible exit angles. We can't afford to do it for more than one collapsar, and neither could they."

She didn't say anything while she filled her cup. "Maybe we've stumbled on their version of Stargate. Or maybe they have more ships than we do by now."

I filled and sugared two cups, sealed one. "No way to tell." We walked back to a table, careful with the cups in the high gravity.

"Maybe Singhe knows something," she said.

"Maybe he does. But I'd have to get him through Rogers and Cortez. Cortez would jump down my throat if I tried to bother him now."

"Oh, I can get him directly. We . . ." She dimpled a little bit. "We've been friends."

I sipped some scalding coffee and tried to sound nonchalant. "So that's where you've been disappearing to."

"You disapprove?" she said, looking innocent.

"Well . . . damn it, no, of course not. But—but he's an officer! A *navy* officer!"

"He's attached to us and that makes him part army." She twisted her ring and said, "Directory." To me: "What about you and Little Miss Harmony?"

"That's not the same thing." She was whispering a directory code into the ring.

"Yes, it is. You just wanted to do it with an officer. Pervert." The ring bleated twice. Busy. "How was she?"

"Adequate." I was recovering.

"Besides, Ensign Singhe is a perfect gentleman. And not the least bit jealous."

"Neither am I," I said. "If he ever hurts you, tell me and I'll break his ass."

She looked at me across her cup. "If Lieutenant Harmony ever hurts you, tell me and I'll break *her* ass."

"It's a deal." We shook on it solemnly.

The acceleration shells were something new, installed while we rested and resupplied at Stargate. They enabled us to use the ship at closer to its theoretical efficiency, the tachyon drive boosting it to as much as 25 gravities.

Tate was waiting for me in the shell area. The rest of the squad was milling around, talking. I gave him his coffee.

"Thanks. Find out anything?"

"Afraid not. Except the swabbies don't seem to be scared, and it's their show. Probably just another practice run."

He slurped some coffee. "What the hell. It's all the same to us, anyhow. Just sit there and get squeezed half to death. God, I hate those things."

"Maybe they'll eventually make us obsolete, and we can go home."

"Sure thing." The medic came by and gave me my shot.

I waited until 1950 and hollered to the squad, "Let's go. Strip down and zip up."

The shell is like a flexible spacesuit; at least the fittings on the inside are pretty similar. But instead of a life support package, there's a hose going into the top of the helmet and two coming out of the heels, as well as two relief tubes per suit. They're crammed in shoulder-to-shoulder on light acceleration couches; getting to your shell is like picking your way through a giant plate of olive drab spaghetti.

When the lights in my helmet showed that everybody was suited up, I pushed the button that flooded the room. No way to see, of course, but I could imagine the pale blue solution—

ethylene glycol and something else—foaming up around and over
us. The suit material, cool and dry, collapsed in to touch my skin
at every point. I knew that my internal body pressure was increasing rapidly to match the increasing fluid pressure outside. That's
what the shot was for; keep your cells from getting squished between the devil and the deep blue sea. You could still feel it,
though. By the time my meter said "2" (external pressure equivalent to a column of water two nautical miles deep), I felt that I was
at the same time being crushed and bloated. By 2005 it was at 2.7
and holding steady. When the maneuvers began at 2010, you
couldn't feel the difference. I thought I saw the needle fluctuate a
tiny bit, though.

The major drawback to the system is that, of course, anybody
caught outside of his shell when the *Anniversary* hit 25 G's would
be just so much strawberry jam. So the guiding and the fighting
have to be done by the ship's tactical computer—which does most
of it anyway, but it's nice to have a human overseer.

Another small problem is that if the ship gets damaged and the
pressure drops, you'll explode like a dropped melon. If it's the internal pressure, you get crushed to death in a microsecond.

And it takes ten minutes, more or less, to get depressurized
and another two or three to get untangled and dressed. So it's not
exactly something you can hop out of and come up fighting.

The accelerating was over at 2038. A green light went on and
I chinned the button to depressurize.

Marygay and I were getting dressed outside.

"How'd that happen?" I pointed to an angry purple welt that
ran from the bottom of her right breast to her hipbone.

"That's the second time," she said, mad. "The first one was on
my back—I think that shell doesn't fit right, gets creases."

"Maybe you've lost weight."

"Wise guy." Our caloric intake had been rigorously monitored
ever since we left Stargate the first time. You can't use a fighting
suit unless it fits you like a second skin.

A wall speaker drowned out the rest of her comment. "Attention all personnel. Attention. All army personnel echelon six and
above and all navy personnel echelon four and above will report
to the briefing room at 2130."

It repeated the message twice. I went off to lie down for a few
minutes while Marygay showed her bruise to the medic and the armorer. I didn't feel a bit jealous.

* * *

The Commodore began the briefing. "There's not much to tell, and what there is is not good news.

"Six days ago, the Tauran vessel that is pursuing us released a drone missile. Its initial acceleration was on the order of 80 gravities.

"After blasting for approximately a day, its acceleration suddenly jumped to 148 gravities." Collective gasp.

"Yesterday, it jumped to 203 gravities. I shouldn't need to remind anyone here that this is twice the accelerative capability of the enemy's drones in our last encounter.

"We launched a salvo of drones, four of them, intersecting what the computer predicted to be the four most probable future trajectories of the enemy drone. One of them paid off, while we were doing evasive maneuvers. We contacted and destroyed the Tauran weapon about ten million kilometers from here."

That was practically next door. "The only encouraging thing we learned from the encounter was from spectral analysis of the blast. It was no more powerful an explosion than ones we have observed in the past, so at least their progress in propulsion hasn't been matched by progress in explosives.

"This is the first manifestation of a very important effect that has heretofore been of interest only to theorists. Tell me, soldier." He pointed at Negulesco. "How long has it been since we first fought the Taurans, at Aleph?"

"That depends on your frame of reference, Commodore," she answered dutifully. "To me, it's been about eight months."

"Exactly. You've lost about nine years, though, to time dilation, while we maneuvered between collapsar jumps. In an engineering sense, as we haven't done any important research and development aboard ship . . . that enemy vessel comes from our future!" He paused to let that sink in.

"As the war progresses, this can only become more and more pronounced. The Taurans don't have any cure for relativity, of course, so it will be to our benefit as often as to theirs.

"For the present, though, it is *we* who are operating with a handicap. As the Tauran pursuit vessel draws closer, this handicap will become more severe. They can simply outshoot us.

"We're going to have to do some fancy dodging. When we get within five hundred million kilometers of the enemy ship, everybody gets in his shell and we just have to trust the logistic computer. It will put us through a rapid series of random changes in direction and velocity.

"I'll be blunt. As long as they have one more drone than we, they can finish us off. They haven't launched any more since that first one. Perhaps they are holding their fire . . . or maybe they only had one. In that case, it's we who have them.

"At any rate, all personnel will be required to be in their shells with no more than ten minutes' notice. When we get within a thousand million kilometers of the enemy, you are to stand *by* your shells. By the time we are within five hundred million kilometers, you will be in them, and all shell compounds flooded and pressurized. We cannot wait for anyone.

"That's all I have to say. Sub-major?"

"I'll speak to my people later, Commodore. Thank you."

"Dismissed." And none of this "fuck you, sir" nonsense. The navy thought that was just a little beneath their dignity. We stood at attention—all except Stott—until he had left the room. Then some other swabbie said "dismissed" again, and we left.

My squad had clean-up detail, so I told everybody who was to do what, put Tate in charge, and left. Went up to the NCO room for some company and maybe some information.

There wasn't much happening but idle speculation, so I took Rogers and went off to bed. Marygay had disappeared again, hopefully trying to wheedle something out of Singhe.

We had our promised get-together with the sub-major the next morning, when he more or less repeated what the commodore had said, in infantry terms and in his staccato monotone. He emphasized the fact that all we knew about the Tauran ground forces was that if their naval capability was improved, it was likely they would be able to handle us better than last time.

But that brings up an interesting point. Eight months or nine years before, we'd had a tremendous advantage: they had seemed not quite to understand what was going on. As belligerent as they had been in space, we'd expected them to be real Huns on the ground. Instead, they practically lined themselves up for slaughter. One escaped and presumably described the idea of old-fashioned in-fighting to his fellows.

But that, of course, didn't mean that the word had necessarily gotten to this particular bunch, the Taurans guarding Yod-4. The only way we know of to communicate faster than the speed of light is to physically carry a message through successive collapsar jumps. And there was no way of telling how many jumps there were between Yod-4 and the Tauran home base—so these might be just as passive as the last bunch, or might have been practicing infantry tactics for most of a decade. We would find out when we got there.

The armorer and I were helping my squad pull maintenance on their fighting suits when we passed the thousand million kilometer mark and had to go up to the shells.

We had about five hours to kill before we had to get into our cocoons. I played a game of chess with Rabi and lost. Then Rogers led the platoon in some vigorous calisthenics, probably for no other reason than to get their minds off the prospect of having to lie half-crushed in the shells for at least four hours. The longest we'd gone before was half that.

Ten minutes before the five hundred million kilometer mark, we squad leaders took over and supervised buttoning everybody up. In eight minutes we were zipped and flooded and at the mercy of—or safe in the arms of—the logistic computer.

While I was lying there being squeezed, a silly thought took hold of my brain and went round and round like a charge in a superconductor: according to military formalism, the conduct of war divides neatly into two categories, tactics and logistics. Logistics has to do with moving troops and feeding them and just about everything except the actual fighting, which is tactics. And now we're fighting, but we don't have a *tactical* computer to guide us through attack and defense, just a huge, super-efficient pacifistic cybernetic grocery clerk of a logistic, mark that word, *logistic* computer.

The other side of my brain, perhaps not quite as pinched, would argue that it doesn't matter what name you give to a computer, it's a pile of memory crystals, logic banks, nuts and bolts . . . If you program it to be Ghengis Khan, it is a tactical computer, even if its usual function is to monitor the stock market or control sewage conversion.

But the other voice was obdurate and said by that kind of reasoning, a man is only a hank of hair and a piece of bone and some stringy meat; and no matter what kind of a man he is, if you teach him well, you can take a Zen monk and turn him into a slavering bloodthirsty warrior.

Then what the hell are you, we, am I, answered the other side. A peace-loving, vacuum-welding specialist *cum* physics teacher snatched up by the Elite Conscription Act and reprogrammed to be a killing machine. You, I have killed and liked it.

But that was hypnotism, motivational conditioning, I argued back at myself. They don't do that anymore.

And the only reason, I said, they don't do it is that they think you'll kill better without it. That's logic.

Speaking of logic, the original question was, why do they send a logistic computer to do a man's job? Or something like that . . . and we were off again.

The light blinked green and I chinned the switch automatically. The pressure was down to 1.3 before I realized that it meant we were alive, we had won the first skirmish.

I was only partly right.